Married to the
Wrong Man

Married to the Wrong Man

M. Louise Glover McKelton, Goolsby, Martin, Davis
AKA M. Louise Davis

TATE PUBLISHING
AND **ENTERPRISES, LLC**

Published by Tate Publishing & Enterprises, LLC
127 E. Trade Center Terrace | Mustang, Oklahoma 73064 USA
1.888.361.9473 | www.tatepublishing.com

Tate Publishing is committed to excellence in the publishing industry. The company reflects the philosophy established by the founders, based on Psalm 68:11,
"The Lord gave the word and great was the company of those who published it."

Published in the United States of America

ISBN: 978-1-62902-917-7
1. Fiction / General
2. Fiction / Thrillers / General
13.12.26

CHAPTER 1

Married to the Wrong Man

Me'Chell reached into the mailbox and took out the mail. One of the letters was from State College and the others were just junk mail. She tore up the junk mail and put it into the trash can. Eagerly, she opened the letter from the college. A big smile came over her face. She had been accepted to the college. Taking that GED class had paid off for her—it opened the door for her to go to college.

This was a dream come true. All her life that was all she wanted to do: go to college. She was able to get a grant, and now the way had opened up for her to go to college.

Me'Chell did not graduate from high school. She was only fifteen when she dropped out of school. Me'Chell was a slow learner, and she lost interest in school. Shortly after dropping out of school, she got married. The marriage only lasted three years—just long enough for her to have three babies. Pauline, her daughter, was the oldest. Then came Mike, and a year later, she gave birth to Tim.

She was a single young mom with three babies. Her job kept a roof over their heads and food on the table, but she wanted more out of life. She was really just a child herself when they separated. It was a struggle trying to raise three babies while living on the edge of poverty. She had a low-paying job making five dollars an hour, taking care of the flowers and plants at Whitewater Technical Plant. This was a mega company. Me'Chell had to walk almost a mile to the plant after getting off the bus. Her baby was now ten years old and in the fifth grade, and the oldest was thirteen years old and in the seventh grade.

Me'Chell began to put things in prospective. *I will have to work at night or see if I can work part time. I can't afford to give up my job. I wish I could get a car. It would make getting around so much easier.* There was no way Me'Chell could afford to buy a car. Me'Chell talked to her boss, and he let her work part time. She went to classes on Mondays and Wednesdays and worked Tuesdays, Thursdays, and Fridays from 7:00 a.m. to 3 p.m. Pauline had been helping her mother by getting the children off to school. Me'Chell left for work at 6:00 in the morning, and she got home around 5:30 in the evening. Her schedule did not have to change.

When Me'Chell had a lot on her mind, she would go for a walk or create a praise dance. This day while walking, she met two ladies that were walking their dogs. The older lady's name was Martha Lewis, and the other lady's name was Betty White. Me'Chell and Martha became good friends, and Betty became her best friend. Martha and her mother were heavily involved in campaigning for politicians. Me'Chell often went out with Martha and her mother campaigning and canvassing for politicians. Me'Chell and her new friends often went walking together.

Sometimes they would pass by Alfie's Limo Co. *It must be nice to be able to rent one of those limos and go somewhere special*, she would say to herself. One day, when Me'Chell walked by the limousine company, the owner was standing in the door. She smiled. He smiled back. "You have a nice business, and you have everything looking so nice. Your business dresses up this neighborhood," she said.

"Thanks," he responded.

Me'Chell did not realize that her new life would be the beginning of a life full of nightmares. But everything seemed to fall right into place. She found a friend to take her to the college, and she enrolled for winter classes at the college. Me'Chell thought that after her tuition was paid, the rest of the money would come to her, and she would use that money for transportation and for things she would need for her classes.

She had a little money coming in from child support. Several months went by, and she had not heard anything from the college about the money she thought she would be getting. Now she was using money that was to take care of her family and for bus fare to go to college.

Trying to go to college had put unexpected heavy burdens on Me'Chell. She did not want to stop going to college, and she cut back on spending money every way she could. Me'Chell began to get stressed out. *I need to relax. This is too much coming at me.* Me'Chell turned on the radio and "My Heart Say Yes" by Troy Sneed was playing. She began to dance. She danced to drown out her worries.

One day while Me'Chell was waiting for the bus to take her to work, she thought she would freeze. It was the coldest day they they have had all winter. Seeing the bus coming up the street brought thoughts of warmth to her mind. But when she got to her destination, she could only think of how cold that long walk to the plant would be. As she stepped off the bus, a cold breeze caressed her, sending chills through her body. She had only walked a short distance when a car pulled up and stopped. The man in the car asked if she was going to the plant.

"Yes, I am," she answered.

"I am going to the plant myself, and I can give you a lift if you like. I believe it is the coldest day we have had this year," he commented.

"I would love that. It is a little chilly out here this morning," she responded with a shaky voice.

"My name is Thomas," he said.

"And my name is Me'Chell," she replied.

Most of the time, Thomas would get to the bus stop shortly after Me'Chell got off the bus, and he would give her a ride up to the plant. He started inviting her to his house. Thomas's house was huge. It had five bedrooms, a big living room, dining room, kitchen, and patio off the family room. Each room had its own bathroom, and it also had a Florida room. The house sat on five acres of land. When he drove up to the house, the garage door opened, and at the back of the garage was a large laundry room. Thomas lived thirty miles from Me'Chell.

Sitting inside of the garage was a new Mercedes-Benz. Thomas was a retired colonel and had two children:

a boy and a girl. His daughter was married, and his son was in the twelfth grade. Thomas had a masters degree in engineering. He was the CEO at the plant.

This man was smart. Me'Chell was a freshman and not so smart, but she was trying to better herself by going to college. This was the beginning of a long friendship. Thomas was nice but somewhat distant. Me'Chell did not have any idea where this relationship was going.

When Me'Chell graduated, she became unhappy with their relationship. *I might not be as smart as Thomas, but I have gone through a lot of hard times trying to go to college. No, I did not have fine clothes to wear, but I did study hard, and I did graduate from college. I am working hard to better myself, and this man makes me feel like I am not good enough to be his girlfriend. Well, I guess if he feels that way about me, he really wouldn't want me for his wife. I am not going to keep sleeping with this man if I am just someone to relax his muscle when it gets hard.*

Me'Chell turned on the radio. The song "Order My Steps" by Women of Worship was playing. Me'Chell moved the table in the living room and began to create several dance steps. Her children came into the room. "What do you call that?" Pauline asked.

"It is my creation. Why? You don't like them?" Me'Chell responded.

"Let me show you what a creation is," Pauline stated. She began to create some dance movements. The song ended. The next song played was "I Choose to Worship" by Wess Morgan.

"If that is the best you and Mom can do, let me and Tim show you some movements," Mike said. The two boys danced like a swan, with great precision. Me'Chell and Pauline joined the boys, and they choreographed a praise dance, a family dance of love and praise.

Most of the summer was depressing for her, and she wanted to be more than the woman Thomas slept with. *I am not getting any younger. All I am doing is wasting my life away messing with that Thomas. I have given him four years of my life, and he still acts like I am not his girlfriend.* Me'Chell began to catch the early bus to work so she would not run into Thomas. She was not able to get her full-time job back.

It was time for the children to go back to school. The summer was approaching fall. Pauline was now in the twelfth grade, Mike was in the eleventh grade, and her baby boy was in the tenth grade. It seemed like time was moving by so fast, and she was going nowhere.

One day, Me'Chell decided that she would call Thomas and find out where she stood in his life. She picked up the phone. She had only seen Thomas three times during the summer.

"Thomas, where do I stand in your life? Do I have a future with you?"

"Me'Chell, I am not ready for a serious commitment," he told her.

"I guess that answers my question. That's all I wanted to know." Me'Chell hung up the phone. That was the last call Me'Chell made to Thomas. After she hung up the phone, she went for a walk.

Thomas was now out of Me'Chell's life. *No more calls and no more visits. Since he didn't want to commit to me, he is out of my life. I should have realized that when he introduced himself to me as Thomas—his last name, not his first name*

Phil. All this time, he has never asked me to call him by his first name, she told herself.

One day Me'Chell went walking by herself; she noticed some new limousines sitting in the lot of the limo company. These were prettier than the old ones. *These limousines must be new. I don't recall seeing them before. One of these days, I am going to rent a limo and drive all over town.* She was admiring one of the limousines when the owner came out and spoke to Me'Chell.

"Hello. You like that limousine?

"What? Why would you ask me a question like that?" she asked. "I can't buy it."

"I did not ask you if you wanted to buy it. I asked you if you like it."

"Yes, I think it is pretty."

"Would you like to go for a ride in it?"

Me'Chell looked at him and laughed.

"Where in the world would I go in a limousine?"

"I would take you anywhere you wanted to go."

"Pardon me, are you asking me on a date?"

"Yes, I am."

"I don't know you."

"But I know you. I have seen you lots of times walking by. I know you live a few blocks over and you have three children. I know all of your kids. I know that you went back to school and got your GED and then went to State College. I know your name is Me'Chell Green, and by the way, my name is Alfie. I admire you for trying to better yourself, and I would like to get to know you better. I also know that you and your children love to do praise dances."

"Yes, I will go out on a date with you."

"How about this weekend?" he asked.

"How about six o'clock Friday evening? I guess you know my address too."

"Six this Friday evening, and yes, I know your address."

Me'Chell later began to think about Alfie. She was stunned that this man knew all about her, and as many times as she had walked by this place, he never said anything to her. *I wonder how long he has been talking to my children. Maybe I'd better find out more about this Alfie fellow. And to think I said I would go on a date with him!* When the children came home from school, Me'Chell called them into the living room.

"I met the man today that owns the limousine company. He told me that he knew you all, and this man knows all about my business. What have you all been telling him, and what do you all know about him?"

"Mom, he is nice. Everybody likes him, and you should try to meet him. He would be good for you. Oh, you did say you met him today. I wonder what took so long for you two to meet. I think he likes you. Every time we go by there, he always asks how you are doing," Pauline stated.

"I know that you all are old enough to stay by yourselves, but I am going to get Betty to sit with you this weekend. I have a date with the limousine man."

Me'Chell called Betty. "Betty, I know you might think I am being silly, but I need a sitter to stay with the kids while I go on a date Friday evening at six o'clock. I just would feel better if a grown person was in the house with them in case I want to stay out late."

"Girl, you know I would love to sit with the children. You have some good children, and I like being around them," Betty told her.

Me'Chell called Martha after she finished talking to Betty.

"Martha, you know that limo place we pass by when we are walking? Guess what! He asked me for a date! Yes, he is good looking, but that isn't why I am going to let him take me out. I have been lonely for so long, and it would be nice to have some fun for once. You have noticed him watching me? You've got to be kidding. The first time we walked by? You think this man has liked me all this time? He has never said anything to me. You could be right. I think this is the first time I went walking by myself. Sure, I would love to go canvassing with you this week. I just love being around your politician friends. Tell Mom I said hello."

Working only three days a week gave Me'Chell a lot of free time, and most of that time she spent with Martha and her mother campaigning for politicians.

Friday evening the children were sitting on the couch watching Me'Chell get ready for her date.

"You would think Mom had never been on a date before, the way she is acting," Tim said.

"Tim, Mom has to look her best tonight. That is why she is rushing around like a chicken with its head cut off," Pauline stated. They all started to laugh.

"Okay, I know you all are laughing at me. I don't remember when I have been out on a real date, and yes, I do want to look my best. So stop laughing at me. All this is new to me."

After Me'Chell had gotten dressed, she came in the living room and stood before the children.

"Now, how do I look? Do I have the Green family stamp of approval?"

"Mom, you look great," they all said.

Me'Chell sat on the couch with the children. The doorbell rang. Me'Chell got up and opened the door. It was Betty.

"My, don't you look good," Betty said as she entered the house. They all sat on the couch and talked, waiting for Me'Chell's date to show up. They wanted to see if he was going to pick her up in a limousine and which one he would be in.

"I hope he picks Mom up in that new white limo," Pauline said.

"I like the black one best," Mike said.

"Wait a minute. Who said he was going to pick me up in a limo?"

"Mom, he is the limousine man. He'd better pick you up in a limo and take you out in style, or I will have to tell him off the next time I see him," Pauline stated.

"You really think he is going to pick me up in a limo?"

"Yes," they all said.

When Me'Chell told the kids about her date, they were all happy. Now they were eagerly waiting to see their mother go on a date with the man that owned the limousine company. He was to be Me'Chell's knight in shining armor.

At six o'clock sharp, they heard a car pull up in front of the house. The children and Betty raced to the window.

"We told you he was going to pick you up in a limo. He is in the white one!" Pauline called out.

Alfie got out of the limousine, dressed in a black suit, a white shirt, a black tie, and black shoes. He looked sharp! Me'Chell saw him come up to the steps. *My, does he look good*, she thought. She waited until he knocked on door; then, she opened it.

"Hello," she said.

"It is six o'clock, and your knight in shining armor is here," he said.

"Have a good time!" the kids called out to her as she was being escorted to the limousine. Me'Chell's neighbors got their eyes full. Me'Chell knew she was going to be the talk of the neighborhood.

He had one of his drivers driving the limousine. He opened the bar in the limousine.

"What would you like to drink?" he asked.

"Do you have any ginger ale?"

"Is that all you drink?"

"I don't drink alcoholic beverages."

"Then I will pour both of us some ginger ale."

He turned on some slow jazz. He looked at Me'Chell and smiled.

"You look so lovely tonight. Is there anywhere you would like to go?"

"No. I will leave that up to you. You seem to know everything about me. Let's see if you know what I like."

After riding for an hour, the limo pulled up at the 500 Lakeside Country Club. Near the club was a river and a big white ship called the *500 Cruise Ship*. The driver got out and opened the door for Alfie; then, he walked around the limousine and opened the door for Me'Chell. Alfie escorted Me'Chell to the *500 Cruise Ship*. It was big, beautiful, and it was three decks high. The rooms on the first floor were set up for private parties or with just you and your guest. This was too much for a first date. "What's on the second floor?" Me'Chell asked.

"Lots of people and lots of noise," Alfie answered

"Sounds like that would be lots of fun. Let's go upstairs," Me'Chell suggested. This night was made for lovers sailing down the river. The full moon lit up the night as the stars twinkled like diamonds in the sky. The music was mostly soft, and the food was indescribably delicious.

They ate, danced, talked, laughed, and watched the stars, heaven's bright lights. Me'Chell leaned on the ship rails, and Alfie put his arm around her as they stood there, hypnotized by the beauty of the night. On the last dance, he sang softly to her. The song was "I Found Love" by Be Be Winans/CeCe Winans. The ship was back at the dock, and everyone was getting off.

"Did you enjoy yourself?" Alfie asked

"Yes. I don't know when I have had such a wonderful time," she answered.

In the limousine, Alfie leaned over like he was going to kiss her. Me'Chell leaned back on the seat. He took Me'Chell's hands and kissed them.

"Can I see you again?" he asked.

"Yes."

Me'Chell wrote her phone number on a piece of paper. "Do you already know my phone number, or do I need to give this to you?" she asked, holding up the paper.

"Yes, I do know your phone number."

"You know, this is kind of scary. You know too much about me."

"Your children love to talk about their mother. And you take some nice pictures."

"You don't think my children were trying to set me up with you, do you? I know they were happy when I told them I had a date with you. I am not looking for a lover. You can call me tomorrow if I have made myself clear."

"That is fine, and I still want to call you tomorrow."

The night had to come to an end, and the limousine was pulling up in front of Me'Chell's house. Alfie got out and helped Me'Chell out of the limousine. He walked her up to the door and kissed her on the forehead. "Good night. Thanks. I had a wonderful time tonight," Me'Chell said softly.

"I am the one that is thankful about you letting me take you out tonight. You don't know how you have made my night. I will call you tomorrow," he responded.

Me'Chell walked into the house and closed the door. She leaned back onto the door. "What an evening. Is he for real, or am I dreaming? This man treated me like I was a queen. He did not try to push me or rush himself on me," Me'Chell muttered.

Betty said, "You gotta tell me about tonight."

"Tonight, I was a queen, maybe a princess being serenaded by a knight down by the river in the moonlight."

Me'Chell lay in bed that night and daydreamed about her knight in the moonlight cruising down the river and dancing under the stars. Me'Chell was awakened by the kids jumping on the bed.

"Tell us about your date last night," Pauline said.

"I was a princess last night sailing down the river in a beautiful white ship with a handsome, sweet prince."

Me'Chell looked at the clock on the wall. "Oh my goodness! It is eight o'clock! I have to get up and fix breakfast."

"Mom, we already ate. I guess your date wore you out. Go back to sleep," replied Mike.

Me'Chell got up and took a shower and got dressed. She went into the kitchen and was sitting at the table eating when the doorbell rang. She got up and went to the door.

"Who is it?" she called out.

"Forever Yours Flower Shop. I have some flowers for Ms. Me'Chell Green."

She peered out the window, and sure enough, there was a young man standing at the door with some flowers.

She opened the door, took the flowers, and smelled them. "Hmm. Thanks! Wait a minute." She got her pocketbook and took out four dollars and gave it to the young man.

She got a vase and put some water in it. Me'Chell put the vase with the flower on the cocktail table. "Now who sent them to me?" She looked at the card stuck in the flowers. It said,

> Take time to smell the flowers. It is a wonderful world out here. Signed, Miss you.

I bet Thomas sent them to me. I have not called or seen him for some time. If he thinks sending me flowers is going to make me call or see him, he has another thing coming. Shortly after the flowers arrived, the phone rang.

"Hello? Hi! Yes, I had a wonderful time last night. Well, I am going to be busy tonight, but later in the week maybe. The flowers? Yes, I got the flowers, and they are beautiful. Thanks! What did I do to get flowers? You are kidding! You think I am that sweet? I have only known you for a few weeks, and I think dating two nights in one week is a little too fast for me. Yes, I love the flowers, and

I had a wonderful time last night. I tell you what—I will come around to your company tonight. I would like to get to know you better. You know so much about me, and I don't know anything about you. What did you mean by you miss me?"

"Every minute I am away from you, I miss you," he explained.

A few hours later, Me'Chell went for her walk. When she walked by Alfie's Limo Company, Alfie was standing in the door. Me'Chell walked over to the door. "Do you ever do any work? Every time I walk by, you are standing in the door."

"I have this built-in radar that tells me when you are coming this way," Alfie said, with a look of passion in his eyes. Me'Chell's eyes met his, and she felt weak in the knees.

"It was nice seeing you again. I guess I'd better get home," Me'Chell stuttered.

"I thought you said that you would stop by and get to know me better."

"I stopped. So I am going home now. Anyway, I said this evening." Me'Chell was anxious the whole day about going over to see Alfie. *I wonder if I should go over there. I feel so weak when I get around him. This man could really hurt me. I think I am falling in love with him.* Me'Chell's mind was saying, *Don't go,* but her heart was saying, *Go, girl.* By four o'clock, she had the children fed and had taken a shower. She came downstairs in a black pant suit, a white blouse, and white shoes.

"Where are you going? You are all dressed up," Pauline asked.

"I am not dressed up. I am just wearing a pant suit."

"Mom, did you look at yourself in the mirror? You look good. That is not just a pant suit. It is a pant suit that is hugging you," Pauline commented.

"I am just going to walk around to Alfie's. I promised him I would stop by this evening. It is five o'clock, and I'm going to leave now. I won't be gone long."

As Me'Chell was walking up the street, she could see Alfie standing in the door. She walked up to him.

"Hello. How are you doing?" she asked.

"I am okay," he answered.

"I don't know why I asked you that crazy question. I can see you look fine. Now that I have seen you, I will go home," she blurted out.

"You have to come in. I am not doing as well as I look. My day has been rough. You can come in for a few minutes, can't you? I promise I won't bite you."

"Why would you say that?"

"Say what?"

"Are you trying to be funny? I don't know why you would say you would not bite me."

"Because you are acting like I am going to bite you or something. You are shaking. Do you feel all right? Let me help you inside. I think you need to sit down for a while and get yourself together."

"I am together. A couple of thoughts just ran through my mind. I was not ignoring you. I was just thinking about something that happened today. I don't think you are going to bite me. I have no fear of you."

"Then come into my parlor, as the spider said to the fly."

Me'Chell went inside, and Alfie closed the door. He put up the Closed sign in the window of the door. Alfie took Me'Chell by the hand and led her into the back of the store. There were flowers all around the room. In the center of the room was a table set for two.

Alfie had the room set for an elegant evening. He pushed a button on the wall, and some soft music echoed through the room. He took Me'Chell into his arms and started to dance. His body felt so good to Me'Chell, and she laid her head on his chest. An hour had passed, and they were still dancing. They had danced all this time without saying a word. Me'Chell looked up at Alfie and said, "I need to get home."

"I know," Alfie remarked.

"Did you notice anything about the room?" Alfie asked.

"Yes. You have everything just right. I love the flowers. Are you expecting someone to come over and have dinner with you?"

"I did all this for you, Me'Chell."

"Alfie, I don't know what to say."

"You being here dancing with me said everything."

Then he kissed her on her right cheek. "I will walk you to the door."

Me'Chell was dumbfounded. This man was getting her emotions all worked up. He fixed up this room for a romantic evening. And what did he do when she said she had to go? He kissed her on the right cheek and walked her to the door.

"This man is playing some kind of mind game with me. I need to back away from him for a while," Me'Chell muttered as she walked home. Me'Chell's feelings for him were growing strong, but things were moving too fast for her. She was not ready to fall in love with anyone, but this man was blowing her mind. She felt like she should stay away from this man. She had to stay strong and fight this feeling of desire for him.

Me'Chell turned on the radio when she got home, and the song playing was "I Worship You because of Who You Are." Me'Chell started to dance, trying to relax her mind from the man who was blowing her mind.

The next day, Alfie called Me'Chell. Pauline answered the phone. "Mom, the phone is for you!" she called out. Me'Chell picked up the phone.

"Hello? Oh, hi, Alfie. I was looking through the paper for a job. No, I don't want to come and work for you. I would not get any work done. Alfie, I really like everything you did yesterday. You are a very romantic person, and one day you are going to blow some young woman's mind. You hope that young woman will be me? Alfie, I like you—I really do, but I am not ready for a serious relationship right now. I just finished college, and I am trying to put my life back together. Yes, we can be friends. Yes, I can go out sometimes with a friend."

Every day Alfie and Me'Chell talked on the phone. He would play his favorite songs. I Found Love When I Found You and Be Still by Yolanda Adam as they they talked. Two weeks had passed since Me'Chell had been at Alfie's business. Every week Me'Chell would find an envelope with a hundred dollar bill in her mailbox. She would call Alfie and ask him why he was leaving money for her. "Why do you think it was me who left the money?" he asked.

"I can't think of anybody else, and this money thing started right after I went out with you."

A month had passed when Alfie asked Me'Chell if he could come over that night. "Make it around seven o'clock. I should be finished with what I have to do by then. And don't come in a limousine. I don't want to blow my neighbors' minds."

Me'Chell did all her chores. During dinner, Me'Chell was sitting at the table smiling.

"What are you so happy about, Mom?" Mike asked.

"If you have to ask Mom a question like that, you are dumber than I thought you were. Look who's been taking Mom out and calling her. Where did he take her when they went out on that date? And what did she tell us? She went sailing down the river with a prince," Pauline remarked.

"Now, kids, guess what—Alfie is coming over tonight around seven o'clock, and I want you all to be on your best behavior."

Me'Chell thought seven o'clock was never going to come. At seven o'clock, the doorbell rang. She peeked out the window from behind the blinds.

"Seven o'clock on the nose. I wonder what's with him getting here right on time. He is always right on the nose."

Me'Chell opened the door. You are right on time. Come on in. Don't pay me any mind. I feel like joking tonight."

"I am fine, and how are you? Alfie replied.

"I can see you are fine. What did you do, buy out the store? Let me help you with all these bags. Let see, three pizzas and two big bags." Me'Chell looked out the door as she took the pizza.

"What are you looking for?" Alfie asked.

"I was wondering how you managed to get all this stuff from the car to the door." Me'Chell shut the door and put the pizza on the cocktail table.

"Those bags look heavy. You did not have to buy all this stuff."

The kids came into the room and started going through the bags and pulling out their contents.

"I didn't know what kind of pizza you all like, so I got cheese 'cause most children like cheese pizza. Then I got chicken and vegetables in case you are trying to keep your shape, and then I got the works with all the goodies in case you want to live dangerously."

The kids took chips, candy and soda, napkins, paper plates, and cups from one of the bags and put them on the cocktail table.

"You thought of everything," Me'Chell said.

"I tried to," remarked Alfie.

"We emptied one bag. Now let's see what's in the other bag," Pauline said. Me'Chell and Alfie stood back and watched the children destroy the second bag. It was full of games and movies; they were having the time of their lives.

Me'Chell took Alfie in the kitchen. "Come with me, Alfie. I am going into the kitchen to get some ice."

"Alfie, you shouldn't have bought all this stuff. The kids are going to be expecting something every time you come over."

"Did you say every time I come over? Does this mean I can come over often?"

"You know what I meant. I was talking about when you do come over. Yes." Me'Chell blushed. She got an ice bucket and filled it with ice. She smiled and handed the bucket to Alfie. They went back into the living room.

"Okay, who wants what?" Me'Chell called out. The house was filled with joy and laughter. Pauline put one of the games under her blouse and looked at the clock. "It is getting around our bedtime. I guess we should go upstairs and get ready for bed." The other children looked at her like she was crazy. Pauline's head nodded toward the clock as she slightly closed one eye.

"Oh! It is about that time," Mike and Tim said, yawning.

The children got up and went upstairs. The room became quiet.

"They've never volunteered to go to bed early before," Me'Chell remarked.

"You got some smart children," Alfie replied.

Alfie picked up a tape.

"This is a very good movie, a little sweet and a little sad, but a great story. *A Summer Place*—have you seen it?"

"No, but I heard that it was a good movie."

"I do have some other movies."

Alfie picked up two other tapes. "This one is scary, and this one has a lot of shooting in it," he commented.

"*A Summer Place* will be fine." Me'Chell put up the games and put the tape in the tape player. Me'Chell sat down next to Alfie on the couch, and he put his arms around Me'Chell, pulling her closer to him. Me'Chell leaned her head on his shoulders. Every now and then, Alfie would look at Me'Chell. He saw tears in her eyes. He pulled out a handkerchief and gave it to Me'Chell. "I told you it was a great movie," Alfie said.

"No, this is not a great story. It is a great love story," she answered. Alfie kissed Me'Chell on the forehead. Me'Chell looked up at Alfie. He turned his head toward the television and finished watching the movie. *Wow, this man is smooth,* Me'Chell thought. Me'Chell sat up and looked at Alfie.

"You are an amazing man. A girl could get used to this."

"As long as you are that girl."

Alfie stood up and took Me'Chell hands, pulling her up from the couch. Their eyes met. Alfie said, "Me'Chell, I had a lovely evening. You have a wonderful family, and I hope that we can do this again soon. I would love to take you and the children out to dinner and a movie real soon."

"We would love that," Me'Chell answered.

Alfie pulled Me'Chell close to him and kissed her gently on her forehead and said, "It is getting late, and I think I should be going."

"You always leave me speechless. What's up with you?"

"If you let me take you out tomorrow, I will tell you."

"Two nights in a row? Well all right."

Alfie started toward the door.

"Wait, let me get your games and movies."

"Give the games to the kids, and I will take the movies you don't like. Will seven o'clock tomorrow evening be too late for you?"

"No, and I will keep *A Summer Place.*"

"Wear something 'after-five' tomorrow," he told Me'Chell.

Alfie picked up the other movies, winked at Me'Chell, and walked out the door. *This man is trying to blow my mind.* Me'Chell sighed, closing the door and leaning up against it. The day seemed to pass by very slowly for Me'Chell. She looked at the clock. It was only four o'clock in the afternoon. The kids were outside playing, and they came running into the house.

"Mom, you have a package."

"Where did you get this package?" she asked.

"A man in a flower truck brought it." Me'Chell opened the box. It was a big vase shaped like a champagne glass, with baby's breath and twelve beautiful silk red roses.

"Mom, these are the prettiest roses ever," Pauline said.

"You think these roses are from Alfie, don't you? I know that you all like him, and I like him too. Now let's see if there is a card in this box."

"Mom, the card is on the roses. See? There is a little gold ring attaching to the card, and it is from Alfie."

Pauline handed the card to Me'Chell, and she read it. She smiled and handed the card back to Pauline.

"Now put it back in the glass."

"I told you all this was from Alfie, didn't I?" Pauline blurted out to her brothers.

"Go wash up. I would like to feed you all your dinner early so I can get the kitchen cleaned by 5:30."

"Why, Tim asked?

"Why what?" Me'Chell asked.

"Why do you want us to eat early?" Tim asked.

"I have something to tell you. Alfie is taking me out again on a date, and it is tonight. Betty is going to baby sit you all tonight at her house. Before you ask why we are going to her house, it is because she can't come over here tonight. I could not find anyone else in such a short time."

Me'Chell returned home after dropping off the children at Betty's. She laid out the clothes she was going to wear and took a soothing, sweet-smelling bubble bath. After she got dressed, she went downstairs and watched television.

An hour had passed when Me'Chell heard a car parking in front of her house. She got up and looked out the window. *That's a pretty car*, she thought. *That man got out of that car, and he is coming up to my door. I don't know him*, she thought. The doorbell rang. Me'Chell opened the door.

"Yes?" she said.

"I am looking for a Ms. Green."

"I am Ms. Green. May I help you?"

"Yes. Alfie sent me to pick you up and bring you to him."

"Why would he send you to pick me up?"

"It is a privacy thing."

"Where is he?"

"He is at the club."

"Okay."

Me'Chell got her purse and closed the door. The man took her arm and escorted her to the car. He opened the door and helped Me'Chell into the front seat of the car. Me'Chell felt her neighbor's eyes looking at her. The driver got in the car. "Now my neighbor is going to think I am dating two men."

They finally reached the club. Me'Chell could see Alfie standing on the steps. He walked over to the car and opened the door for Me'Chell and escorted her into the club. He took her to a private room. It was beautifully decorated—even the table was decorated. Alfie pushed a button on the wall, and soft jazz echoed around the room, sounding like a live band, was sitting around the room. This was music for lovers. Alfie pulled the chair out for Me'Chell. She sat down in the chair.

He pushed it up to the table. A waiter came and served the table. "I hope you will like what I picked out for us to eat."

"How could I not like T-bone steak?"

The waiter came back with a bottle of sparking white grape juice. He opened the bottle, and it popped just like champagne. He poured some in the glasses. Me'Chell picked up her glass.

"Sparking white grape juice?"

"Yes. I don't want you to get drunk," he said and winked.

"What's up with you always winking your eye?"

He got up from the table and stretched out his hand to Me'Chell.

Me'Chell got up. Alfie walked toward her and pulled her into his arms and started to dance.

"I will show you."

"What are you going to show me?"

"Everything you have been wondering about me."

They danced over to the wall and Alfie pushed a button and a door opened. It was an elevator. They danced into the elevator. The door closed. They never stopped dancing. He was dancing slow and smooth, holding her close to him. The door of the elevator opened. They danced into a room prettier than any room she had ever seen. There were three rooms: a Florida room, a bedroom, and a living room. Alfie was holding Me'Chell close to him, and he kissed her on the forehead. "I kissed you on the forehead out of respect for your children. I winked my eye at you because of what I planned for you, and I wanted everything to be perfect when I make love to you." Then he kissed her on the lips.

"You were so sure of yourself."

"Yes. You want me. I planned it that way. I don't just want your body. I want you to love me."

"In the closet, there are some things you can change into. I don't want you to wrinkle you dress." Me'Chell open the closet door and saw a sexy night gown and a dress. *If I put on the gown, I am saying I want him to make love to me, and if I put on the dress, it is saying I am not ready to make love to him.*

Me'Chell took one of the garments and went into the bathroom. Me'Chell looked around in the bathroom. The bathtub and sink were made of white marble trimmed in gold. The style of the bathroom looked like it was made for a Greek goddess. There were several bottles of sweet shower gel sitting on the sink. Me'Chell picked up each bottle and smelled them. She founded one she like and rubbed it on her arm. She smelled her arm. *This really smells good. I would like to smell all over like this. I could lather myself up and rinse off. I don't know. It might give him the wrong idea.* She lathered herself down with the apple blossom shower gel. then rinsed off in the shower. She walked out of the bathroom smelling like apple blossoms, and went back in the room. Alfie had changed his clothes and was sitting on the couch waiting for her. He looked at Me'Chell.

"I thought you would pick that." Me'Chell walked over to Alfie and kissed him. He picked her up and put her on the bed. He took her left foot and kissed it. And he started to suck her toes; then, he did the same with her right foot. He kissed her legs, her knees, her thighs, her navel, her breasts, her neck, and then her lips. Yes, Me'Chell had picked the night gown.

Me'Chell felt a sensation that went from her feet through her whole body that made her feel like she wanted to explode. Me'Chell was lying in Alfie's arms and thought, *I have to be dreaming. None of this is real. Nothing good ever comes my way.*

"What are you thinking?" Alfie asked.

"I was thinking that you are an amazing person. You did all this just for me. You have to be a very caring person. I wished I could have met you when I was sixteen years old. Just think how different my life could have been."

"Let me show you something," Alfie said as he got up and pulled Me'Chell up from the bed. He took her into the Florida room. There was a big, white mink blanket on the floor under a tree full of sweet-smelling flowers. Alfie pushed a button on the wall. The ceiling began to open. The whole ceiling opened up, and they could see the moon and stars in the sky. They lay down on the blanket.

Me'Chell lay in his arms. "Listen to the music, and relax your mind. See how beautiful the stars are shinning. You see that big star in the sky? It is shinning the brightest. That star is my star to you, and one day, I would like to put a star on your finger that shines like that. She lay in his arms listening to the soft music for lovers and watching the stars.

"Is there anything you like to listen to?"

"I love Johnnie Mathew's 'It's Not for Me.'"

Alfie picked up a remote and pushed some buttons.

"The next tape you hear will be the great Mr. Mathews."

He pulled the blanket over them.

"I knew it," he said.

"You knew what?"

"You have a lot of love burning in you. I could tell it in your walk, your voice, and your smile. It was inside of you waiting to be cultivated and harvested."

"Did my loving Johnnie Mathew have anything to do with what you just said?"

"That and more."

He kissed Me'Chell passionately on the lips. Me'Chell closed her eyes, put her arms around his neck, and kissed his back, blocking out the world. Me'Chell had never had anyone make love to her like this, making her feel so complete. She was lying in his arms looking up at the sky.

"Alfie, look! There are shooting stars in the sky."

"Did you make a wish?"

"Yes."

"Can you tell me what your wish was?"

"No."

Alfie and Me'Chell lay under the tree wrapped up in the mink blanket, watching the stars and listening to music for lovers.

Me'Chell was awakened by a kiss on her lips, like a prince awakening his princess. Everything was so loving and peaceful that she had fallen asleep.

"Good morning," Alfie said

"Morning." Me'Chell started to get up. Alfie leaned over her and kissed her again.

"Wait. I want you to see the sunrise. Have you ever watched the sunrise?"

"No."

"I will get you home before your neighbors get up."

"You want to bet on that?"

"No."

The golden ball was slowly pushing up through the darkness of the night. Alfie kissed her hands. Then he took each one of her fingers and sucked them as they laid wrapped in mink with music for lovers echoing around the room. The air had the smell of a flower garden.

"I have to get home. I will never forget this night, Alfie."

Me'Chell got up and took a shower and put her dress on.

She came out of the bathroom, and Alfie was dressed.

"Is there another bathroom room in this place?"

"Yes. There are two bathrooms in the apartment."

He pushed another button on the wall, and the wall opened wide enough to reveal a tray with two breakfasts on it.

"I really need to get home."

"It is not even 5:30! I will have you home by 6:30. It is not going to take you but a few minutes to eat something."

"Okay."

After they had finished eating, they got on the elevator and went though the restaurant to the lobby. The fellow who had brought Me'Chell to the club was waiting for her.

"Call me when you get home," Alfie said.

"Okay."

The fellow helped Me'Chell into the front seat of the car.

She began to daydream about the night she just had and could not believe all that had happened to her. It was like being a princess for the night. The next thing Me'Chell knew, she was home. The driver got out and opened the door for Me'Chell and helped her up the steps.

Me'Chell got her keys out of her purse and opened the door.

"Come in," Me'Chell says to the driver.

"No ma'am."

"I just want to give you a tip."

"No, thank you ma'am. Everything has been taken care of. Good day, ma'am."

Me'Chell shut the door. "My, he is a weird man. Every other word is ma'am."

Me'Chell went upstairs and changed her clothes. She came back downstairs and called Alfie.

"Were you sleeping? I made it home safe and sound. Your driver was very polite. You know I did. I had the best time of my life. Sure you can call me tonight."

Me'Chell laid down on the couch and went to sleep. She was awakened by the phone. It was Pauline.

"Mom, what time are you coming to get us?"

Me'Chell looked at the clock. It was 8:00 a.m.

"I will be over in about an hour."

"Mom, Ms. Betty said she would bring us home after we eat breakfast."

"Okay."

Me'Chell turned on the TV. *Good Morning America* was on. "Let me see what they are talking about today," Me'Chell said as she laid down on the couch. An hour had passed when Betty brought the children home.

"Come walk me to my car," Betty said.

Me'Chell knew what she wanted. *I can't tell her everything that happened last night*, she thought.

Me'Chell walked Betty to her car.

"Get in the car. You have to tell me everything."

"You've got to be kidding. Well, he had a driver to pick me up, and he took me to that 500 Country Club. We had a private dinner. We danced under the stars and moonlight. This place was like something out of a fairytale. He was so romantic. Girl, I just can't explain it. I felt like a princess being swept away by her knight. It was unbelievable. That is about the best way I can explain it."

"Wow! That said a lot. I got the idea of it all."

"Betty, thanks for taking care of the children for me. I don't want them to know I was out all night."

"Any time you need someone to watch the children when you go out, just call me. I am home alone most of the time, so I enjoy any company." "Thanks again," Me'Chell said as she headed into the house.

"Mom, what were you and Ms. Betty talking about for such a long time?" Mike asked.

"She was telling me how bad you all were."

"We were not bad. Tim was the loudest, but not bad," Pauline said.

"I was just kidding. She said that she loves watching you."

"It should not have taken that long to say she loved watching us," Mike said.

"You are right, and we did some girl talk."

"Was it about you going out last night?" Tim asked.

"Yes."

"Tell us about last night."

"Well, I went out with a friend, and we had a great time. I had been stuck in the house so long I'd forgotten what it was like to go out and have a nice time. I am not talking about the time Alfie took me out. I really enjoyed that night."

Me'Chell called Alfie and told him she would like for him to meet her mother when he got off work. She gave him her mother's address. The children were still in school. She fixed them something to eat and left a note on the kitchen table telling them what she had fixed for their dinner, also that she would be at her mother's house. When Alfie got to her mother's house, she had fixed dinner for them. They all sat down at the table and ate. They had a good time, talking and laughing. Alfie took Me'Chell home. He did not want her to catch the bus back home.

The time slowly passed by. Alfie called Me'Chell at 3:00 p.m.

He wanted to take Me'Chell and the children out to dinner.

"Do you think taking you and the children out for dinner tonight would be too soon to see me again?"

"Alfie, that would mean we would have spent three nights in a row together."

"As far as I am concerned, we can spend every night together," Alfie told Me'Chell.

"Tomorrow is Sunday. Going out for dinner tomorrow would be nice."

"Does that mean I can't see you tonight? You do like being with me, don't you?

"Yes. You don't have to ask a question like that. Okay, we can go out tonight for dinner. What time do you want us to be ready?"

""I will pick you and the kids up at five thirty. Will that be okay?"

"Yes. We will be ready."

Like always, he was right on the nose. At 5:30, the doorbell rang, and it was Alfie. Me'Chell called the children.

"Alfie is here to take us out to dinner."

"Mom, you have had a lot of company this week—three nights in a row! Mom went out last night with a friend," Tim said.

"You don't say. Who did she go out with?" Alfie inquired.

"It was a friend," Tim said.

"I think we'd better leave before we end up not going anywhere," Me'Chell spoke out.

"Where would you kids like to go?" Alfie asked.

"We love Chucky Cheese." They all said.

"Then your wish is my command."

Alfie took them to Chucky Cheese, and the children had the time of their lives eating all kinds of pizza and playing games.

"You were trying to be funny tonight, asking the kids who I went out with last night."

"Not really. I just want to know what they were thinking."

After they finished eating, he took Me'Chell and the children home. As Alfie was coming up the street to Me'Chell's house, she could see Thomas's car sitting in front of her house. *Oh no*, she thought. Alfie pulled up in front of Thomas's car.

Me'Chell said, "Thanks, Alfie, I will see you tomorrow."

"Okay," he answered.

Alfie pulled off, and the children ran into the house. Me'Chell walked over to Thomas's car. "What are you doing here?"

"You stopped calling and coming to the house."

"Thomas, I have found someone else, and I don't want you anymore." Me'Chell had been seeing Alfie for around two and half months, and he had been good to her and her children. He had faith in her and made her feel important. Every week, he would put a hundred dollar bill in an envelope and put it in her mailbox.

Thomas drove off, but the first thing the next day, Thomas was knocking on Me'Chell's door. Me'Chell was still in bed sleeping. "Who in the world can that be at my door?" She looked at the clock. "It is only 6:00 a.m." Me'Chell went to the door.

"Who is it?" she called out.

The voice from behind the door said, "Thomas."

Me'Chell opened the door.

"What are you doing here so early in the morning? Especially when I told you I did not want to see you anymore."

"Me'Chell, I love you," he said. Then he looked on the coffee table and saw the roses. He picked up the card and read it. A look of anger came over his face. Thomas took the glass of roses and threw it at the wall. Glass went all over the floor.

"What is wrong with you? You can't come to my house and destroy my things."

"I am sorry. I love you, and I just can't live without you."

Me'Chell was picking up the broken glass from the floor. Thomas ran into the kitchen. "I am going to kill myself!" He started rummaging through the drawers, looking for a sharp knife. This caught Me'Chell off guard. *This man is talking about killing himself, and he is in my kitchen looking for a knife. What in the world am I going to do?*

"Thomas, look. We have to talk about this. I can't think right now. I have a doctor's appointment. You will have to leave, but I will call you, and we will talk."

"You will call me when you get home?"

"I will call you as soon as I can, Thomas."

⌒⌢⌒⌢⌒

"What am I going to do? I don't want this man's blood on my hands."

The kids came downstairs. "Mom, what was all the noise about? We thought we heard Thomas," Pauline said.

"You did hear Thomas. He was here for a few minutes."

"Mom, you don't look good. What did Thomas do to make you look like this?"

"Look, Pauline, Mom's roses are on the floor, and there is glass on the floor," Tim commented.

"Yes, Thomas broke my pretty glass and messed up my roses."

"Mom, I am glad you stopped going over to his house. He gives me the creeps," Pauline said.

"We don't like him. He doesn't seem like a nice person," stated Tim.

"I was going to fix you all some pancakes, but I don't feel good. Eat some cereal. After I clean up this mess, I am going to lie down."

Me'Chell got all the glass cleaned up. She lay down on the couch and tried to relax. Her nerves were shot. All she could think about was Thomas saying he was going to kill himself. Me'Chell picked up the phone and called Martha.

"Martha, you will never believe what happened to me this morning. Thomas came by first thing this morning.

He threw my beautiful roses that Alfie gave me up against the wall and broke the glass they were in, and he said he was going to kill himself. He ran into the kitchen and was looking for a knife. That's not funny. I do not have two men fighting over me.

"Martha, if Thomas killed himself, I would not be able to live with myself knowing he died because of me. I don't know what to do. What do you mean you can't find one fellow to fight over you? I thought you and that lawyer you went out with last month were getting tight. I have to go. You are no help to me. I have to call Alfie and talk to him."

Me'Chell hung up the phone. *What am I going to say to him? I have an old boyfriend talking about killing himself if he can't have me. That sounds so corny.* Me'Chell picked up the phone and dialed Alfie's number.

"Alfie, I have a problem, and I need to talk about it. Can I see you after you finish work? Okay, I will come around closing time."

There was a knock at the door. Me'Chell went to the door and opened it. Thomas was standing there.

"What are you doing here? I told you I would call you after I came back from the doctor."

Thomas came into the house. "I came to ask you to marry me." He had this one and a half carrot ring, and he put it on Me'Chell's finger. Me'Chell looked at the ring.

"Thomas, I can't give you an answer right now. I will have to call you, and we can talk about it."

Me'Chell started to take the ring off her finger. "Don't take the ring off. Me'Chell, I can't live without you. I will come back when you call me with an answer."

He left Me'Chell speechless, standing in the middle of the floor and looking at the ring. Me'Chell had no plans to call Thomas, and now he had left her with a guilty feeling.

Me'Chell went over to Alfie's company after the closing hour. Alfie had left the door unlocked for Me'Chell, and all his workers had gone home. She opened the door and went into his office. He looked at her, and he could tell something was wrong. "Wait here. I want to lock up so we can talk without interruptions."

Me'Chell had her hands in her pocket. She still had not taken off the ring. Alfie took Me'Chell into his arms and said, "You look like you have some bad news to tell me. The pretty smile I am used to seeing is gone."

"I am so confused. The fellow I used to go with came to the house and threatened to kill himself if I didn't marry him."

He held Me'Chell close and kissed her. "Me'Chell, please don't fall for this man's lies and tricks. He is not going to kill himself if you don't marry him. That was him sitting in front of your house, wasn't it?"

"Yes."

"He saw you with someone else and could not stand to think that someone else could love you. Me'Chell, I do love you, and I want to marry you myself. Why don't you take your hands out of your pockets?"

Me'Chell took her hands out of her pockets. Alfie looked at her hands.

"You are wearing his ring." He pulled Me'Chell close to him. "Me'Chell, Me'Chell, I love you so much. I was hoping that you felt the same way about me. If you did, you would have told him no."

"You don't understand. He said that he would kill himself if I don't marry him. I would not be able to live with myself if he died because of me."

"Do you love him?"

"No."

"You can't love me, because you are confused. If you loved me, Me'Chell, there would only be one answer. You would only think about your love for me."

A tear came to Alfie's eyes. He stood there holding her and smothering her in kisses, knowing that this would most likely be the last time he would get a chance to hold Me'Chell in his arms.

"I..."

Alfie put his right hand over Me'Chell lips. "I love you too much not to have all of your love."

As Me'Chell started to walk out the door, he said, "Me'Chell, this man is tricking you. He has no intention of killing himself."

CHAPTER 2

I Married the Wrong Man

Me'Chell called Martha. "I am going to call Thomas tonight and tell him to come over. I want you and Mom to meet him." Martha's mother called Me'Chell her adopted daughter. Me'Chell hung up the phone and called Thomas.

"Thomas, you can come over around two o'clock tomorrow, and we will talk."

Thomas was there at two o'clock the next day knocking on Me'Chell's door. Me'Chell called out, "Who's there?" In her heart, she knew that it was Thomas. She had not made up her mind what she was going to do.

"It is me. Thomas."

"Just a minute," she called out

Me'Chell opened the door. Thomas came into the house and sat down on the couch. Me'Chell sat down next to him.

"Thomas, I will marry you."

"We can get married next week. We will have to get a blood test and a marriage certificate. If we get the blood work done today, everything will be ready by next week," Thomas commented.

"I can't get ready by next week. Let me get a calendar and pick out a date. I have some planning to do."

"Okay."

Thomas took his wallet out of his pants pocket and gave Me'Chell $400.

"You should be able to get what you will need for the wedding."

Me'Chell took the money and looked at it. *What is $400 going to buy as high as wedding stuff is?* she thought.

"Thomas, I would like for you to meet some friends of mine: Martha and Mom, her mother." Me'Chell took Thomas over to Martha's house. Martha was looking out the window and saw them drive up and get out of the car. Martha was very impressed with Thomas's car. He was driving a brand-new Lincoln. Martha opened the door for Me'Chell and Thomas as they got out of the car and walked up the side walk. As Thomas and Me'Chell entered the house, Martha and Me'Chell greeted each other with a hug. Martha hugged Thomas also. Mrs. Lewis was sitting on the couch in the living room. Me'Chell walked over to Mrs. Lewis and hugged her. She turned to Thomas and said, "Thomas, this is my adopted family, Martha and her mother, Mrs. Lewis. She is Mom to me."

"It's nice to meet any friends of Me'Chell. Did she tell you that we are going to get married in a few weeks?"

"She said that she might get married some time soon. That is not going to give us much time to plan a wedding," Martha stated.

"You know I was thinking the same thing," Me'Chell stated.

"Girl, I was just kidding. I am going to help you plan everything," Martha replied.

Me'Chell and Thomas had a good visit with Martha and Mrs. Lewis. Martha and Thomas seemed to have a lot in common as they all talked and laughed, and they entertained each other. Me'Chell had not planned on staying long, but the connection Thomas had with Martha and Mrs. Lewis had her staying two hours longer then she had planned.

"Me'Chell, Mom and I will have a small reception here at the house for you, and I have a wedding gown that I bought several years ago. I was supposed to get married, and it fell through. So we have two things taken care of for your wedding," Martha stated.

"Martha, I don't know what to say. That would be a big help to me."

The month flew by fast, and it was the day of Me'Chell's wedding. Thomas had gotten a fellow he worked with to be his best man, and Martha was Me'Chell's maid of honor. Even though it was winter, the sun was shining, and it was a beautiful day but cold. While the wedding was taking place, the weather changed. A storm, a very bad storm, came from out of nowhere. The wind was so strong that trees were being uprooted, and the rain was coming down like a waterfall, flooding the streets. All this happened in one hour's time.

When they walked out of the church, no one could believe how this bad storm could take place in such short time. Me'Chell ran to the car and twisted her ankle getting into the car. Martha had prepared a beautiful wedding reception for the newlyweds at her house.

Thomas had also prepared something at a club. Because of the storm, the club closed early, and Thomas had to have the wedding reception at his house. He had so much food, and somebody had to eat it. A few people went to Thomas's house. They did not let a storm stop them from celebrating Thomas and Me'Chell's wedding.

When they got to the house, Me'Chell showed Tim where he would be sleeping. "This is your room. Since Mike and Pauline are staying with Mom, it is you and me. Thomas's son will be coming home this summer, and I am hoping that you and Thomas's son will be like brothers. Anyway, when Mike comes to stay with us, you all can share the room, or he can have his own room. I don't have to worry about Pauline. She will be going off to college."

Me'Chell changed out of her wedding dress. Even though Me'Chell was in pain, she tried not to show it. Thomas was enjoying socializing with his friends.

Me'Chell was sitting on the couch talking to a lady when Thomas walked over to her and said, "Let's dance." Me'Chell got up slowly, trying not to show the pain her ankle was giving her. She got close to him, and he pushed her back. "We can't be dancing like that."

"What the heck? This man is supposed to be so in love with me, and he doesn't want to hold me close to him?" Me'Chell muttered to herself. So they danced like they did in the old days when a single man and woman would dance. Their bodies could not touch. After they finished dancing, Me'Chell sat back down on the couch. She was in so much pain that the ladies sitting on the couch tried to comfort her.

Me'Chell's ankle was now hurting really bad, and one of the ladies was rubbing her ankle. One of these ladies was named Mary Goods. She was there with her husband. Thomas never showed any love or compassion. He never came over to Me'Chell to see what was going on with her. Then it hit her. *This man doesn't love me. Alfie was right.* Me'Chell realized that she had married the wrong man. She hobbled into the bedroom, lay down on the bed, and started cry.

It was her wedding night, and she was crying—not from the pain she was in, but because she realized this man did not love her; he just didn't want anybody else to have her. It was her wedding night, and she was supposed to be happy. Instead, she was sad and crying her heart out. After a good cry, she hobbled out of the bedroom and sat on the couch and talked to the ladies.

That night was the worst night of her life. That was the way Me'Chell felt. But little did she know that most of her marriage would be pure hell. Thomas had Me'Chell quit her job. He did not want her working at the plant.

The next day when Me'Chell got up, Thomas and Tim were in the kitchen eating cereal. Me'Chell got some corn flakes and a bowl from the cabinet and sat down at the table. Tim had finished eating and excused himself from the table.

"Good morning," she said.

"I don't see anything so good about it," Thomas replied.

"You don't sound like a man that just married the love of his life," Me'Chell said.

"Did you sleep with that man?"

"What are you talking about?"

"The fellow whose car I saw you getting out of."

"Whatever I did was none of your business. After all, I was nothing to you, and I was never your girlfriend. When I was seeing him, I was not seeing you. I had broken off any relationship I had with you."

"If I had known you had slept with him, I would have never married you. I asked you, did you sleep with him!"

Me'Chell got up from the table and went back to bed.

"Why? Why didn't I follow my heart and marry Alfie? What this man has for me is not love but possession. I was never good enough to be his girlfriend, and when he saw me with someone else, he couldn't stand the idea that another man was in my life. He doesn't want me, and he doesn't want anyone else to have me," Me'Chell said to herself.

The first day of her marriage was a cold one, but the second day was not any better. Pauline was in the twelfth grade and did not want to change schools. Mike was in the eleventh grade and was not ready to change schools, because the school year would end in three months. Pauline and Mike wanted to stay with Me'Chell's mother until school ended. Her mother lived in their school district and near a bakery that made the best cakes.

Me'Chell wanted to give Pauline a graduation and "going away to college" party. She confronted Thomas with the idea.

"Thomas, I want to give Pauline a party here at the house. She worked so hard in school to keep her grades up, and in the fall, she will be going to Norfolk State University."

"I don't want a lot of people at my house. Why can't you have it at your mother's house?"

"Because this is where I live, and this is supposed to be my home."

Me'Chell went ahead and put together a party anyway at the house. The night of the party, Thomas was pouting and left the house. When Thomas got back home, the party was over, and they had cleaned the house.

Thomas's son's best friend was the son of Thomas old girl friend named Doris. He was sitting in the family room with Doris's son. They were laughing but stopped when Me'Chell walked into the family room. They got up and went outside. The phone rang; it was Doris looking for her son. Me'Chell answer the phone. "Hello?"

"Hang up the phone." It was Thomas's son. He had answered the phone on the patio. Even his son was cold to her. She had to adjust to this marriage of coldness.

A day or so after that, Thomas was in the family room talking on the phone. Me'Chell was in the living room, and she entered into the family room. Thomas had his back to the living room door, and he did not hear or see Me'Chell coming into the family room.

Me'Chell stopped when she heard what Thomas was saying. He was holding the phone with his right hand, and he had his left hand in his pants pocket. He was rubbing his hand around in his pocket.

"Man, she is not my wife. Yes, we are married. My wife is dead. I just married her for necessary things. I got tired of looking for stuff, if you know what I mean."

Me'Chell could not believe what she had just heard. "He married me for necessary things, like sex, cooking, cleaning, washing, and ironing his clothes. It was not because he loved me." Thomas turned around and saw Me'Chell.

"Me'Chell just walked into the room. Okay, man, I will talk with you later."

"You don't have to hang up because I came into the room."

"I don't like people eavesdropping on my conversations."

"I was not eavesdropping on your conversation. I think I will go for a walk around the neighborhood."

Me'Chell called her mother and talked to Mike and Pauline. Pauline and Mike wanted to stay with her mother until the summer was over. Then she went for her walk. She had only walked two blocks down the street. There was a lady standing by a mailbox. Me'Chell walked by her and spoke.

"Hello. It is a beautiful day for walking."

"Yes. It is a beautiful day. I have not seen you in the neighborhood before," the lady said.

"Yes. I am new to the neighborhood. My name is Me'Chell Thomas."

"Then you must be Thomas's new wife."

"Yes, I am."

"My name is Doris. Thomas and I were once great friends. My son and Thomas's son are close friends. I know they were hoping that he and I would make it as a couple, but I could not put up with his ways. Good luck with your marriage."

Me'Chell walked for about a half a block and began to think.

Maybe if I had stopped, she would have told me all about Thomas.

The walk was peaceful. Me'Chell was not ready to go back into the house. She walked up to the house and sat on the porch.

Her mind drifted back to when she overheard Thomas talking on the phone. "So he doesn't think I am his wife. I am just someone for him to have sex with, someone to cook, clean the house, wash and iron his clothes… and to think I gave up Alfie for this man! A man that really loved me and thought I was special! He treated me like a queen," Me'Chell uttered to herself. She became depressed. She got up and went into the house. Thomas, his son, and Doris's son were sitting at the kitchen table. The phone rang. It was Doris. Thomas had answered the phone. She said she wanted to speak to her son. But it seemed like Thomas did more talking than her son.

Me'Chell called out, "I don't feel good. I am going to lie down on the bed. I am sure you all can find something in the refrigerator to eat when you get hungry." She went into the bedroom, laid down on the bed, and cried herself to sleep. The next thing she knew, Thomas was getting into bed."

"You need to get up and put on you gown and get into bed."

"What time is it?"

"It is ten o'clock."

Me'Chell got up and put on her nightgown. *I wonder if I can play like I am so sleepy that he will leave me alone,* she thought to herself.

Me'Chell turned the covers back on her side of the bed. She got down on her knees and said her prayers. She eased into the bed, hoping not to wake Thomas. She pulled the covers up over her.

He pulled her closed to him. A chill swept over her body. She laid still. He started to pull up her gown. She could feel his body getting on top of her, and he was trying to kiss her. This was making her flesh crawl. Me'Chell started to pray. *Lord, please let this be quick.* He had done what he married her for, and she was now thanking God for making it quick.

Me'Chell had only been married a few months and it felt like years. She began to wonder how she was going to make this marriage work—a marriage of no love—and her heart cried out, *Why didn't you listen to Alfie?* A tear came to her eyes. Now all she could do was dream of what love could have been like.

Me'Chell was sitting in the family room one evening, and the doorbell rang. She got up and went to the door. She opened it.

"Hello. My name is May. I am a neighbor of yours. I just dropped by to welcome you to the neighborhood. I am sorry it took me so long to welcome you to the neighborhood."

"Thanks. Come in."

"I have a lemon cake as a welcome gift for you. I hope you like lemon cake."

"Lemon is my favorite cake."

May and Me'Chell became close friends. One day Thomas's first wife came up in the conversation. "Thomas's first wife was very unhappy. She said that she could not take it anymore and was thinking about getting a divorce, but she died of a heart attack soon after that.

Me'Chell met the man that had the house in back of Thomas, and he told Me'Chell that Thomas had a bad temper. He told Me'Chell that Thomas was going with a young lady, and she quit him. The man started dating the lady, and Thomas came over to his house and jumped on him. It seemed like everybody that knew Thomas had nothing nice to say about him.

Maybe I should have met his neighbors before I married him, she thought. Me'Chell was in the family room on the phone talking to her mother. Thomas came in the room. She walked into the bedroom. Thomas tore into the bedroom and hit Me'Chell up against the head. *Wop!* "What's wrong with you?" Me'Chell shouted as she swung back at him. He hit her again, knocking her down to the floor.

A week had passed, and she told Thomas that she was going to go and check on her house tomorrow. Me'Chell looked at Thomas, and all she could see was hate in his eyes. The type of hate that says, "I wish you were dead." Me'Chell thought back, and most of the time Thomas had that same look in his eyes, like she was a piece of trash that he wished could disappear. That night, Me'Chell became sick, and the next day, she was still sick. Several weeks passed by the time she checked on her house. This time, she didn't tell Thomas until that day as he was going out the door for work.

She drove by Alfie's business. He was showing some people the limousines. He looked up as she was passing by. Their eyes met, and tears came to her eyes. When she got into the house, she broke down and cried.

Me'Chell cleared her face and went outside. She got in her car and went home, leaving her heart back with all her tears. She turned on the radio, and the song "I Found Love" was playing. "Yes, I did find love, but I was a fool and let it go."

CHAPTER 3

Just Trying to Survive

The days and nights turned into months, and still the love and compassion never came. Trapped in a loveless marriage, she tried to make it work. Her heart was broken; she was sad and did not want others to know she had made a mistake by marrying Thomas.

Pauline had gone online and signed up for NSU, and they had accepted her. The time had come for Me'Chell to take Pauline to NSU. Me'Chell spent the weekend in Norfolk with Pauline. She took Tim with her.

Me'Chell got Pauline settle in NSU and in an apartment before she return home. One day Thomas's best man at the wedding was taking his family to the circus, and he had five extra tickets. He invited Thomas, Me'Chell, and the boys to go to the circus. Thomas thought it would be a good thing if Me'Chell and Tim went with them. He did not feel good and was going to stay home, and his son was out somewhere. He had given Me'Chell ten dollars to spend.

"Let me have the ten dollars," he said. He took out twenty-five dollars and gave it to Me'Chell.

"Oh happy day! How generous. I have to bring my son Mike home soon. I hope I can find a job first," Me'Chell said to herself.

That night at the circus was fun for Me'Chell though. She could not buy much, but it was nice being away from home.

Thomas had to work night shift for some reason for about a month, and most of that time, he had to work overtime due to some type of survey they were having at the plant.

Thomas and Me'Chell stopped by Martha's one day. They were all sitting in the kitchen. Martha got up and went into the other part of the house, and Thomas got up shortly and went in the other part of the house too. Me'Chell had noticed that they were eyeing each other. *How dumb do they think I am? Thomas is flirting with Martha, and she is flirting back with him. My husband and my best friend are trying to play me for a fool if they don't think I can see what is going on. I guess this will be my last time coming over here. It is a shame that I have to give up my best friend. I know that she has lots of men in and out of her life—even married men, but I did not think she would do this to me,* Me'Chell thought to herself.

Martha came back into the kitchen, and Thomas followed shortly afterward.

"Thomas, we have to leave." Me'Chell told him. "I am sorry, but I have something I need to take care of, and we need to leave now," She told Martha.

School had been out for several months when Me'Chell went to her mother's house and got Mike. Now both her sons were staying with them. This was Mike's last year in school, and Tim was in the eleventh grade. They were living in this big beautiful house in a very nice neighborhood. This meant the schools would be better. Time was passing fast, and school would be starting soon. Me'Chell took Mike to school and got him enrolled.

Thomas and the best man at their wedding started hanging out together. One day, the best man's wife called Me'Chell, and they talked a long time. During the conversation, she told Me'Chell that her husband often worked late—at least that was what he told her—but one night, she called his job, and he was not there.

After hanging up the phone, Me'Chell thought about Thomas. He often worked the evening shift and came home late in the night. This must mean the two of them were out doing something they had no business doing. When Thomas came home, Me'Chell told him about the conversation she had with the best man's wife. His comments were, "You'd better not ever call my job and check on me."

Mike had been in the new school for three months, and he loved it. He and Tim had made a lot of friends. Me'Chell was glad that the boys had made some friends at school, and sometimes, they had sleepovers.

Tonight the sleepover was at one of their friends' house. Me'Chell was glad the boys were not home; she and Thomas got into a heated argument.

"You are no good, and nobody in your family is any good! Even your friend Martha is no good. She will sleep with anybody!"

"My family is just as good as yours, and what do you mean Martha will sleep with anybody? You don't know anything about her. You just met her and have only been around her when I took you to meet her and her mother and then at the wedding. The only way you can know who she sleeps with is if you have been sleeping with her yourself."

"I did not sleep with the tramp."

"The only way you would know anything about her sexually is that you have to have been there. You just met her."

That night when they went to bed, Me'Chell turned her back to Thomas and tried to make It look like she was so tired.

Thomas starting feeling Me'Chell's body. He pulled up her gown and ran his hands up and down her legs. *I feel like I am a sex machine to him. He jumps on it to be jacked off*, Me'Chell thought. He must have guessed what she was thinking because he stopped.

Me'Chell woke up to find Thomas up and dressed. He started the argument where they had left off. Me'Chell got up from the bed and started into the bathroom. Thomas stopped her, and the argument became very heated. Me'Chell thought Thomas was going to hit her. She went into the family room and turned on the television. She was so glad that the boys were away at a sleepover.

When he had gone to work, she went into the bathroom, took a shower, and dressed.

The next day, Me'Chell wanted to go and check on her house. The car was low on gas. Me'Chell asked Thomas for $10 to get some gas. His remark was, "It is not my responsibility to keep you in gas."

Me'Chell went through all her purses and pockets looking for some money to buy the gas. She managed to find $5 in change. *I have to get me a job. If he doesn't think he is supposed to give me money, who does he think is supposed to give it to me?*

Me'Chell pulled up in front of her house. She got out of the car. She looked up the street and saw a car coming. It was Alfie. Her heart skipped a beat. "Please don't let him stop."

Alfie pulled his car up to the curb and stopped. He got out of his car and walked up to Me'Chell.

"Hello. How's life been treating you?" he asked.

"Okay."

"Are you sure? You don't sound like the Me'Chell I know and love."

"I have to go."

"Me'Chell, wait. Something is wrong, isn't it?"

Alfie took Me'Chell's hand. She pulled back. The moment he touched her, she wanted to fall into his arms and lean on his strong body and cry. He let her hand go.

"Me'Chell, I still love you. I won't interfere with your marriage, but if you ever need to talk, or a friend, I will always be there for you."

"Alfie…"

"Don't say anything. Remember, you have a friend."

Me'Chell's heart was hurting as she watched Alfie walk back to his car. She watched the man that really loved her, the man she should have married, walking away. Me'Chell found herself leaning against the door inside the house crying.

The leaves on the trees had all changed colors and were falling to the ground, and snow had covered the earth. Winter had come, and soon spring would be here. Their anniversary was just a few weeks away. Me'Chell was thinking about what she wanted to do for their anniversary. Nothing came to her mind. "What do you do when your marriage was a mistake?" she asked herself. *It is a little chilly out today, but maybe a walk around the block will clear my head.*

Me'Chell walked pass Doris's house, and it was empty. Some children were playing in the yard. They spoke as Me'Chell passed by. "I see Ms. Doris has moved," she said.

"Yes. She moved about a week ago. She bought a house in the Village Lake Estate," one of the children said.

But her kids still came over to the house, and she was always calling, looking for her children.

Doris called the house later that week. She wanted to speak to Thomas. Me'Chell had answered the phone, so she told Thomas the phone was for him. Doris told him his son had gotten her daughter pregnant, and she needed one hundred dollars to pay for the doctor visit. Thomas told her he would get the money for her. He didn't break a sweat or change his tone of voice.

"Me'Chell, my son went off and got Doris's daughter pregnant, and she needs one hundred dollars to pay the doctor bill. Since it is my son's baby, I am going to give her the money so she can go to the doctor. I feel it is part of my responsibility to help with the doctor bill."

"You do what you think you have to do. Do you know what your responsibility is?"

Me'Chell was left feeling empty. She knew she had to find a job and try to get herself together. *I don't ever want to have to ask that husband for any money. He felt like it was his responsibility to give his ex-girlfriend money, yet he feels like it is not his responsibility to give me, his wife, gas money. I hate this marriage.*

Me'Chell made a job out of looking for a job. Then one day, Me'Chell got a call from the Tobacco Company. This was music to her ears. They wanted her to start to work the next day. *I will be able to make my own money and to spend it the way I want. He won't have to worry about me asking him for anything anymore.*

The Tobacco Company was a big company that made cigarettes and had three shifts. Only the first shift was open at that time. Me'Chell was hoping she could get the night shift, giving her less time to be around Thomas.

Me'Chell took Tim over to visit her mother. While there, she went by the Cake Shop on the corner from her mother's house.

"Hello," the owner greeted her.

"Hi. You know you have the best cakes in the world. My mother buys your cakes all the time. I can't make up my mind what I want to buy."

"Take your time. I'm running a little short today. One of my girls is sick and will be off for two weeks." The owner was decorating a cake.

Me'Chell walked over to watch him. "I always wanted to decorate cakes like that. I wish I could."

"It is easy. Watch this. See how I move my hand to make a flower. See? It was easy."

"If you would teach me how to do that, I would come and work for you for nothing while your help is sick."

"You are going to come and work a week or two, free, just to learn how to decorate cakes? When can you start?"

"I will put in for a week or two off tomorrow, and I should be able to start the day after tomorrow." Me'Chell bought a lemon cake and went back to her mother's house.

CHAPTER 4

An Angel Is
Watching Over You

At work, Me'Chell put in for two weeks off and got it. It had been a long time since Me'Chell felt this good. After this week, she would be able to make all kinds of pretty cakes. This was going to be her hobby. She would be able to make something pretty and take her mind off her unhappy marriage.

Me'Chell told Thomas that she was going to go the Cake Shop for a week or two. The owner was going to teach her how to decorate cakes. The day she was supposed to go the shop, Me'Chell's stomach started to hurt. She was sick all that day, but the next day, she got worse; the day after that, she became so weak, and each day, she got weaker.

I know the owner thinks I was lying to him by now, she thought. *This is so funny how I got sick all at once when I was to go back to my old town. It's like some kind of spell has been put on me. I'd better get up from here and go back to work.* Me'Chell went back to work, and all the weakness and stomach pains left.

A few days later, Me'Chell was sitting in the family room watching the television. Thomas came into the family room, and the television changer was lying face down. The next thing she knew, she and Thomas were arguing about the television changer. *Whatever he had to say, he could have said it in a nice way, not coming in here and arguing with me,* Me'Chell thought. It seemed like everything she did was wrong, and there was no way she could please him.

It was Sunday, and Me'Chell was awakened by Thomas saying something to her. He must not have liked the way she answered. He jumped up out of bed.

"I can't get no respect around here." He went into the bathroom and took a shower. He was dressed when he came out. "I don't know why I can't get any respect in my own house. I'm going down to the river."

"Look, you don't have to start an argument to go wherever it is you want to go. Just go. When you want to get out of the house, you start an argument."

"I don't need an excuse to go anywhere. I am the man of the house. I am king in my house. You are the one that likes to hang out in the streets."

"The only place I go is to work. It is very seldom I go to visit my mom or check on my house. All I have ever been to you is a substitute wife."

As he was going out the door, he stopped and went back into the bedroom.

"Don't take any of my cars. If you want to go somewhere, you can walk."

It was late in the evening when Thomas returned home.

Me'Chell didn't say anything to him. She looked up from the book she was reading. He looked happy. *I guess he did whatever it was he had planned on doing today. I hope I don't get some kind of disease before I leave this man. I am. I have to get out of this marriage. I am tired of being unhappy.*

That week they had only had two arguments, and that was a good week. Me'Chell was talking to her mother on the phone about her insurance, and Thomas overheard her.

"What? Your mother doesn't have any insurance? Who is going to bury her? Tell your mother I will pay for the insurance. She needs insurance so she can have a nice funeral." Some insurance company had sent Thomas some information about their insurance. Me'Chell called her mother back.

"Mom, Thomas said he would pay for some burial insurance for you so you would be able to have a nice funeral when your time come to pass over. Okay, I will tell him what you said. We can come over, and you will sign the papers."

"Thomas, Mom said that we can come over, and she will sign the insurance papers."

"It is still early. We can eat, and the boys can clean up the kitchen. After we eat, I will take you to your mother's house."

"Okay."

After dinner, Me'Chell put on her black leather coat, and she was wearing her blue leather boots. Thomas took Me'Chell over to her mother's. Everything started off nice. Somewhere, everything got turned around. Her mother was mad.

"No! I am not going to sign any insurance papers. I'll let the person who gets my house bury me." Then out of nowhere, she started to talk about Me'Chell and Alfie.

"Yes, she brought him over here. She fixed him dinner."
She went on and on about Alfie. Me'Chell's heart
wanted to stop. She knew that she would have a big
blowout with Thomas when they got home. *Why is
this woman that calls herself my mother doing this to me?*
Me'Chell looked at Thomas. She could see that he was
mad. He took all he could from her mother, staying only
to get all the dirt he could on Me'Chell. Thomas got up.

"I think it is time for us to leave."

Thomas was quiet as they got into the car. He was
driving down the expressway when he started banging on
the steering wheel.

"You fixed dinner for that man at your mother's house?"

He was screaming at Me'Chell. Then he took his hand
off the steering wheel and struck Me'Chell up against her
head. Me'Chell knew they would have it out when they
got home but never guessed it would start on the way
home. *I am not going to sit in this car and let this man beat
on me all the way home. I have to get out of this car.* Thomas
was doing about fifty-five miles per hour. In her mind,
she was thinking, *I have to get out of this car.* She opened
the car door. It must have shocked Thomas; he tried to
slow down. Then it happened. Me'Chell jumped out of
the car. She rolled down the expressway like a ball.

She got up and hopped back to the city. She had no
money and didn't know what to do. She found a quarter
in her coat pocket, and she called Alfie.

"Alfie, you said if I needed a friend you would be there
for me. Did you mean what you said? Okay, Thomas
took me over to my mother's house to take out some
life insurance on her. She ended up telling him about
me taking you over to her house. He got so mad he was

arguing and banging on the steering wheel, and out of the blue, he hit me. I jumped out of the car. I could not stay in that car knowing that he was going to hit me again. Yes, on the expressway. I am at the service station on Lee St."

It seemed like hours, but it only took Alfie twenty minutes to get to Me'Chell. He got out of his car and went up to Me'Chell.

"Can you make it to the car?"

"Yes. I am okay."

"I will take you to the hospital."

"No! Thomas might be there looking for me. I will go tomorrow."

Alfie drove twenty minutes; then, he turned up a road. Me'Chell could see a big mansion inside of a gated area. It looked like it had been dropped in the center of the Garden of Eden. Alfie drove his car up to the mansion. He pushed a button and the gate opened. When they got to the house, he pushed another button, and the garage door opened. He drove the car into the garage. Alfie got out of the car and opened the door for Me'Chell.

He helped her out of the car and into the house. Me'Chell was stunned and wondered whose mansion he had taken her to. They went past a big kitchen and a dining room with a table to feed twenty-six people. A big chandelier hung from center of the ceiling. He took her to a room where there was a lounging couch. He took Me'Chell over to the couch and helped her take off her coat and put it on a chair.

"I want you to lie back on this couch and try to relax."

"Okay."

Me'Chell slowly inched down on the couch, and she looked around the room. It was beautiful, like something out of the *House & Garden* magazine. Alfie took off her boots and laid them on the floor. He then pushed a button, and a door opened on the wall over the couch. Alfie took out a white mink blanket and put it over Me'Chell.

"This place is yours? You have a mansion? It is beautiful."

"Thanks. This could have been all yours."

"Why did you bring me here? You never brought me to your home when I was seeing you. Did you bring me here just to show me what I am missing for marrying Thomas?

Me'Chell got halfway up from the couch with every muscle in her body hurting, but what hurt the most were the words that just came from Alfie's mouth. Me'Chell banged her hands against Alfie's chest, sobbing. Alfie leaned over Me'Chell. She eased back down on the couch. Alfie got down on his knees and took Me'Chell's hands and put them over his heart. He pushed a button and lowered the couch so he could talk eye to eye to Me'Chell.

"I am sorry. I shouldn't have said that. I didn't mean to make you feel bad. Me'Chell, I still love you, and I will always love you. There has not been another woman in my life since I stopped seeing you. You are the only woman who has my heart. Can you feel it? It is beating just for you and you only. It is killing me to see you like this, to know the woman I love is being treated so badly and to be this close to you, knowing I can't hold you."

CHAPTER 5

Regrets

"I didn't realize how much I loved you until my wedding night. You were right. Thomas was not going to kill himself. The minute I said I do, all that love he claimed to have for me went out the window. I spent my wedding night crying, because I realized I had made one of the biggest mistakes of my life. My marriage to Thomas has been nothing but heartaches, mental, and physical abuse," Me'Chell sobbed as she tried to tell Alfie what her life had been like while she was married to Thomas.

Tears were running down her cheeks. The song "I Want to Be Close to You" by the Carpenters echoed from the speakers. Me'Chell held her hand up. "Take my hand, Alfie. Come lie next to me, 'cause all I want is to be next to you." Alfie lay down on the couch next to Me'Chell and kissed her tears.

"If you were not hurt, I would want so badly to hold you in my arms, to caress your body, and to make passionate love to you. But even if you weren't hurt, I would not be able to make love to you. You are a married woman, and I will not be the cause of you breaking your vows. This is breaking my heart to see you like this. Me'Chell, this man is dangerous. He is going to hurt you really bad one day if you don't leave him. He is a control freak, and they are the worst kind of people. He would rather see you dead than for you to be with someone else."

He held her close, and they both cried. Me'Chell fell asleep, and when she woke up, Alfie had fixed her breakfast and had it on a tray. He had put a folding table next to the couch, and he put the tray on the table. By the couch on the floor, Alfie had put a pair of house shoes for Me'Chell to put on near the couch.

"Good morning. I fixed you something to eat. I think you should eat something before you go to the hospital." He pointed to a door. "That is the bathroom. I put a towel and face cloth in there for you to wash off. And the toothbrush in there is new. No one has used it."

Me'Chell went into the bathroom and washed off. She brushed her teeth. There was a comb on the sink. She picked it up and combed her hair. She was sore, but she managed to move around without showing her pain. After she had finished eating, Alfie warmed up the car.

"Me'Chell, are you ready to go to the hospital?"

"Yes. I don't feel like I really need to go to the hospital. If I had broken anything, I would not be able to walk this well."

"I think you should go to the hospital and get yourself checked out and make sure you don't have any internal injuries."

He helped Me'Chell put on her boots and coat. They walked back through the house to the garage. He held her arms as they walked to the car. He stopped and embraced her in his arms. He held her hand and raised up her head so he could look her in the eyes.

"Me'Chell, you have to leave this man. And when you do, don't let him know you are going to leave him. Just walk out. You don't have to live like this, with a man that thinks of you like you are a piece of furniture or something he bought in a store. It is dangerous that he mentally and physically abuses you. I want you to remember I will always be there for you. I will wait for you to come back to me." Then he kissed her on the forehead and helped her into the car.

When he got to the hospital, he let Me'Chell out at the door of the emergency room.

"I am going to park my car, and I will be right back." Me'Chell went inside the emergency room and signed in at the desk. She found a chair and sat down. She had only been there a few minutes when she looked up and saw Thomas standing in the door. She tried to scoot down in her chair, hoping he would not see her. But he did see her, and he walked over to her.

"I have been worried about you and looking for you all night."

Me'Chell looked up and saw Alfie standing in the door. Their eyes met. He smiled and winked as he turned and went back out the door.

Me'Chell's wait was short. They took some X-rays of Me'Chell.

There were no broken bones. She just had a small raw place on her left hip from hitting the expressway. They cleaned it and put some cream and a dressing on the area.

"Miss, you were lucky. You jumped out of a moving car on the expressway. Just the jump alone could have killed you. Then you could have gotten hit by a car. You also put other people's lives in danger, which could have caused a pileup on the expressway. You had an angel watching over you because all you have is an abrasion on your left hip."

Me'Chell began to give thanks that she was wearing her leather coat and boots. She realized that her leather boots and coat broke her fall. As she was rolling over, the leather was like a cushion. When she jumped from the car, she had to land on her left hip, and then she started to roll. Her boots protected her legs, and only the heel of the left boot was smashed up. "I thank you God for protecting me."

Thomas took Me'Chell home. Tim ran up to her.

"Mom, where were you last night? When Mr. Thomas came home without you last night, it had me and Mike worried." Tim questioned her. He could tell something was wrong, but she did not want to tell him that Thomas hit her, and she jumped out of a moving car. These were teenage boys, and she was afraid of what they might do to Thomas.

"I had a little accident and went to the hospital. I fell, but I am okay now."

Me'Chell jumping out of the car must have shocked Thomas. There was peace in the house for two whole weeks. Thomas even suggested they start going to church, and he found a church not for from them. Me'Chell was in the backyard, and she saw May coming out of her house. She walked over toward May's house. They talked about how unhappy she was.

Me'Chell didn't know what to think. Alfie said that Thomas would rather see his wife dead first before he would let her divorce him. Could he have given her something to make her heart bad? She wondered.

Me'Chell went back into the house. Thomas was on the phone in the kitchen. Tim and Mike wanted to go the library. Me'Chell got into the car, and as she was leaving, Doris's children were pulling up in the driveway. Tim was acting funny. He started to say something then changed his mind.

"If you have something to say, don't start and stop," Me'Chell stated.

"I don't want to start anything, but did you see Ms. Doris's kids pulling up as we were leaving?"

"Yes."

"I was on the other end of the phone when I overheard Mr. Thomas talking to Ms. Doris, and she needed some money to pay her phone bill. It was $400, and Mr. Thomas said he would bring her the $400 to pay her phone bill so it won't get cut off. She told him her children were coming over to his house and to wait until they got there. He then said okay. He also told her he would be driving the Lincoln and would drive around her house to the backyard. I didn't really think anything about it until I watched her kids drive up in the driveway."

"You say what?" Me'Chell said, trying to hold back her anger, but the more she thought about it, the madder she got. Me'Chell turned the car around and went back home. Sure enough, Thomas was gone. Now she was really mad.

"I have taken enough off of this man who calls himself the perfect man. All he is doing is thinking I am a fool and that he can treat me any way he wants. There is one thing for sure—I was a fool for marring him and a bigger fool for staying with him."

Me'Chell turned her car around. She wanted to find him. She was determined to find him and his supposed ex-girlfriend.

When I find them, I am going to show them how much of a fool I am. She didn't want to put up with his ways, but she is still after his money. I am stuck with his ways, and she gets the money," Me'Chell thought to herself.

"Where are you going?" Tim asked.

"I have an idea where Doris lives, and I am going to drive out there," Me'Chell answered.

Me'Chell went out to the country and drove around for about an hour. She did not find a house with a driveway that went around the house or to the backyard. She could see that Tim and Mike were getting restless, so she decided she had spent enough time looking for Thomas. The devil had gotten into Me'Chell, and she was fighting mad.

When Me'Chell pulled up in their drive way , Thomas had returned home, and his car was parked in the driveway. Me'Chell got out of the car. Tim got out of the car and ran in front of Me'Chell. Doris's children and Thomas's son were gone. Me'Chell slammed the door behind her.

"What are you doing slamming the door like that? You could have broken the glass in the door. You need to be more responsible." was Thomas remarks when Me'Chell came into the house.

"You have some nerve telling me I have to be more responsible. Where is your responsibility to me? I am your wife whether you want to recognize it or not. Doris is not your responsibility nor is the child her daughter is carrying. How dare you take $400 to that woman to pay her phone bill when I have to go through hell to get any money from you!"

"I don't know what you are talking about. What $400 am I suppose to give to Doris?"

"Don't play me for a fool. I heard you talking to her about the money, and she said that her phone was going to be cut off if she didn't get the money. Then you told her you would give her the money to pay her phone bill. She also told you to wait until her children got here before you came to the house. You then told her what car you would be driving. Do I need to tell you more about the conversation you had with her? Yes, I was on the other line and heard everything. I did not think too much about it until I saw her children pull up in the driveway as I was leaving. I tell you one thing she'd better not call here anymore, and her children can't come over here anymore either."

"I didn't take her any money. I don't even know where she lives. And her children are close friends to my children. You can't stop them from coming over here."

"I am cutting out all this mess. She can't call here anymore, and to make sure she won't have a reason to call, her children will not be able to come here. If you don't think I mean what I said, try me."

There was an address book by the phone that Thomas had all his friends' phone numbers in. Me'Chell picked up the book and searched for Doris's phone number. Finding it, she dialed her number.

"Hello, Doris. This is Thomas's wife. I know that you asked him for $400 to pay your phone bill. And he came out to your house tonight to give you the money. Don't you ever call my house again, and keep your children from my house too. Don't mess with me because I will blow your head off."

Me'Chell hung up the phone and sat down on the couch in the family room. Thomas over heard Me'Chell talking to Doris.

"You can't call people up and talk to them like that, and you can't tell anyone who can and cannot come to my house. This is my house, not yours."

"I tell you one thing—you all better not try me. I said what I have to say, and I meant what I said, and that is that. I am going to get me something to eat, and I am going to bed."

Me'Chell went to Tim's room. Both of her boys were in Tim's room. She asked them if they wanted something to eat. They said yes, so she fixed her and her boys something to eat. After she cleaned up the kitchen, she went to bed. There was a chill in the house all that week. Me'Chell's job and her boys kept her mind busy, not giving her a lot of time to think about Doris and Thomas.

The house was filled with tension. When Thomas talked to Me'Chell, he always talked down to her, making her feel like a nobody. Me'Chell was becoming depressed and moody. She hated this marriage. *I need to get out of this marriage before I go mad*, she thought. *When he talks to me, he talks down to me like I am a nobody.* A week had passed, and Me'Chell was in bed watching television. Thomas came in the room and got in bed. He got close to Me'Chell. She acted like he was not even there. He put his hands across Me'Chell's stomach and began to pull up her gown. A chill ran through her body as he kissed her. The next thing she knew, he was on top of her doing his thing. Me'Chell believed that a woman should not refuse her husband sex as long as he was not being a sex addict.

This was something she said she would never do. But it was getting harder and harder for her, plus it didn't seem to matter too much now. She felt abused in her loveless marriage. The next day, she made an appointment with a lawyer to talk about getting a divorce from Thomas. She was given an appointment for 3:00 p.m. the next day. All that day, all she could think about was getting free from the mess she had gotten herself into.

Me'Chell was at the lawyer's office. She was escorted to a room. The lawyer came in shortly after she was put into the room.

"How may I help you?" he asked

"I want to get a divorce from my husband."

"Tell me why you want to get a divorce."

"He has been both mentally and physically abusive toward me."

"Explain what you mean by mental and physical abuse."

Me'Chell began to explain how Thomas had treated her. The lawyer looked at Me'Chell and said, "You need to go home and work on your marriage. This man has put you in a beautiful home. He is taking care of you. Do you know how many women wish they had somebody to take care of them?"

Me'Chell could not believe her ears. *This is supposed to be the best divorce lawyer in town, and he is telling me to go back to Thomas and take his abuse!*

CHAPTER 6

Deceiver

It was Sunday morning. Thomas was already up and had taken his bath when Me'Chell got up.

"I can't get no respect around here," he stated.

"What are you talking about, Thomas?"

"I said that the chair at the head of the table belongs to the man of the house. I am the man of the house, and nobody is supposed to sit in my seat."

"What are you talking about?"

"I came home last night, and your oldest son was sitting in my seat at the table."

"You were not home when he sat in the chair. He never sits in that chair when you are home."

"I'm not going to church today. I think I will go to the river where I can relax and get some peace of mind," he stated with an angry voice.

"Thomas, you don't have to start an argument to get out of going to church. You are a grown man. You can do whatever you want without starting a fight."

Me'Chell called the boys so they could get ready to go to church. Thomas's son did not want to go. Me'Chell got her boys up.

"Take your shower, and eat some cereal for breakfast. I am going to fix a big Sunday dinner today," she told the boys.

After she had taken her shower and gotten dressed, she went into the kitchen. Her boys had already started on their breakfast.

"I see you all are almost finished eating. I won't be long. It does not take me long to eat a bowl of cereal."

Thomas had already left and gone to the river. He says that the river is peaceful and makes him relaxed. He likes to go there whenever he gets angry.

Thomas's son was still in bed when Me'Chell and the boys went to church. When they got back, he was gone, and Thomas had not gotten home from the river.

Me'Chell baked a roast, some corn bread, cake, mashed potatoes, and some greens. Me'Chell had finished cooking, and she looked at the clock. It was 5:30.

"It is 5:30 in the evening, and Thomas still has not gotten home. It was around 8:00 this morning when he left, and he thinks I am going to believe he's been at the river all this time."

Me'Chell set the table. "I am going to wait until six o'clock, and if he and his son are not home by then, we will go ahead and eat."

Me'Chell cleaned up her mess and put the food on the table.

"It is six o'clock. Come to the table so we can eat."

Me'Chell heard the front door open. It was Thomas. He walked in the kitchen.

"You all could not wait until I got home before you started to eat?"

"I finished cooking some time ago, and I did not want the food to get cold. Anyway, you have been gone all day, you did not call, and I did not know when you were going to return. So you don't have anything to complain about."

"I am not hungry. I will eat later."

He went into the family room and turned on the television, and stretched out on the couch and went to sleep. His son got home shortly after he did. After the boys finished eating, Thomas's son went in his bedroom and watched television. Me'Chell put the food in the refrigerator and cleaned up the kitchen. Her boys went outside to play.

That night when she got ready to go bed, Thomas was already in bed and seemed to be sleeping. She was hoping that she would not wake him. Me'Chell eased into bed, trying not to wake him. She got as close to the edge of her side of the bed as she could get. She could feel his hands reaching for her. She could not make-believe she was asleep. She had just gotten into bed. Me'Chell's head started to hurt. She felt his hands pulling her gown up.

"I have a headache," she said as she pulled down her gown.

Thomas turned over to his side of the bed and went to sleep. Me'Chell lay there in bed and thought of how unhappy she was in this sham of a marriage. *I hate this marriage*, she thought. The next day brought a brand-new day of adventures. They were off to work or school. That evening when everybody was home and had eaten, they went into the family room and watched television. Me'Chell had just gone into the bedroom when the phone rang.

"It's for you, Mom!" a voice called.

Me'Chell picked up the phone.

"Hello? Hi, Mrs. Goodes. You say what? You saw me and Thomas yesterday in a green mustang on your way to the beach? You waved, and I did not respond? I don't know what to say. Are you sure it was me? If I had seen you, I would have waved back. Did anyone else see him? Your brother-in-law saw him too?"

Now Me'Chell knew what Thomas did when he went to the river. He went to see some women. Already lonely and depressed, Me'Chell confronted Thomas about being with this lady. Of course, he denied it.

Later in the week, Me'Chell got another call. This lady had seen Thomas one Sunday with someone whom she thought was Me'Chell. "Oh, by the way, Me'Chell, I didn't get a change to wave to you a few Sundays ago. I was on my way back from the airport from picking up my husband when you and Thomas passed by us," was what this lady on the other end of the phone said to Me'Chell. The conversation continued, but Me'Chell's mind had drifted. Finally, the phone call came to an end.

Already depressed, she felt this was the dynamite placed on the fire that caused the pot to blow up.

She was so mad she could feel the pressure building up in her. Thomas had gone outside on the patio and was relaxing in the lounge chair. The sun was going down. He was enjoying watching the sun sinking below the horizon as the cool breeze caressed his body. Me'Chell went to the patio and opened the door.

"Thomas, were you on the expressway on Sunday?"

"No, I was at the river all day Sunday."

"Well, I just got a call from a friend of mine, and she said that she saw you and some lady whom she thought was me."

Me'Chell lit in on him. The hurt and hate came out with words of bitterness and detest. If he had been with someone, he was not going to admit it to her. All she did was make him mad.

"You need to stop hanging around people that don't have anything to do but make up lies about people."

"Nobody is making up lies about you. I knew you were deliberately starting fights on Sundays to get out of going to church with me, and now I know why."

"I don't have to make excuses for anything I do. I am grown, this is my house, and I am the king in my house. I am the man around here. I wear the pants in this house." It was another night of coldness in the house. When it came time to go to bed, Me'Chell hated it. She had to climb in bed with this man full of deceit. There was no telling what kind of disease he might bring home. All kinds of negative things ran through her mind. The edge of the bed seemed to be Me'Chell's favorite spot to sleep.

The morning rose with the sun bursting up from the darkness and bringing forth its light and heat. This heat and light shined on Me'Chell's face from between the lines in the window blinds. It had been a long and sleepless night for Me'Chell. She could not get it out of her mind how nasty Thomas was and the stories coming in about him being seen with some woman. The one good thing about the night was that he slept all night.

That morning, Me'Chell got up, showered, dressed, and went to work. At work, it seemed like the end of her shift was never going to come. Finally, it was time to get off work. "I don't know which is worse: working at a job where there is a lot of harassing going on or going home to a husband that despises you." When Me'Chell got home, the children had left a note. Her two sons and Thomas's son had gone to the park. Me'Chell was in the kitchen fixing dinner. She had only been home for a short time when the phone rang. She answered it. It was a woman on the other end.

"May I speak to Thomas?"

"I am sorry. He is not here. Do you want to leave a message or leave your phone number? I will give him the message and have him call you when he gets home."

"My number is 767-9877. Tell him Jean called."

"Okay. I will give it to him as soon as he gets home."

When Thomas got home, Me'Chell gave him the phone number.

"What's this?"

"It's Jean's phone number. She called and wanted to talk to you. She said something about you all being together yesterday."

Thomas took the number and picked up the phone. He dialed the number.

"May I speak to Jean?"

Most of his conversation was filled with the words you use when you don't want people in the room to know what you are talking about. Then he hung up the phone.

"Oh, that was a lady who had been waiting for hours for her boss at work. He was in some kind of meeting. It was around lunch time, so we went to lunch together."

"You think I am some kind of fool, don't you?"

"What is wrong with you, woman? You're acting like I have to get permission for the things I do. Don't forget that I picked you up out of the gutter and gave you a beautiful home and security. All you do is nag me. There are a lot of women that would be glad to have what I have given you. I deserve better than this. I am a businessman, a retired colonel, I am well off, I am not a bad looking man, and I am well educated. I deserve a woman of my standards—a well-educated woman."

"I didn't ask you to marry me. In fact, I told you that I had found somebody and didn't want to see you anymore. If you felt this way about me, why didn't you leave me alone so I could have married someone who loved me and thought that I was special?"

Me'Chell stormed out of the kitchen. She went out to the patio and lay back in a lounge chair. She closed her eyes and began to daydream about Alfie—how he loved her and made her feel special. She was daydreaming about all the good times they had together. She made-believe they were at the club out on the lawn dancing in the moonlight as their hearts beat as one. She thought about his gentle kisses and the night they made love all night long. She thought of the song "I Found Love." *Yes, I did find love, but I was a fool and gave it up.*

Me'Chell began to feel sorry for herself. *To think I had a man that thought the world of me, and I gave it up because this man I married said he would kill himself if I did not marry him. The love he had for me only lasted until I said, "I do." I waited all my life to find someone to love me and my children, and when I did, I threw it away. Alfie, I need you so badly.* Me'Chell's heart was crying. She could only lay there and dream of what she could have had. Me'Chell fell asleep, and when she woke up, everyone had eaten, and the children had cleaned up the kitchen. Me'Chell went into the kitchen and fixed herself something to eat, but her heart was broken. She was unable to eat. She went into the bedroom and went to bed. That night, she cried herself to sleep.

The running of the water in the shower woke Me'Chell. She raised her head up from the pillow and looked at the clock. It was five o'clock in the morning. *I can get a half-hour sleep before I have to get up for work.* She tried to go back to sleep but couldn't. Thomas came out of the bathroom.

"Good morning," he said.

"Good morning, Thomas."

Me'Chell got up and went into the kitchen. The children were eating breakfast.

"Good morning, everyone. You all are eating cereal. I can fix you all some pancakes if you want them."

"We are just about finished eating. You can fix us some tomorrow morning," Mike said.

"Mom, are you all right?" asked Tim.

"Yes. I am fine."

"You don't act like it. I can't remember the last time I saw a smile on your face. You look down in the dumps all the time," Tim commented.

Me'Chell went back into the bedroom and took her shower and got dressed. When she came back into the kitchen, the children had gone to school, and Thomas had gone to work. *I have to do something. I can't keep going on like this. Even the children notice that something is wrong.*

CHAPTER 7

Fear-Stricken

One day, on the way home from work, Me'Chell stopped by the flower shop and bought a plant. She put it out on the patio. The next day, she noticed there was some yellow powder on the soil in the flowerpot. She thought nothing of it. Then one day she noticed there were some mushrooms growing in the flowerpot, and they were yellow. *I have never seen any yellow mushrooms before.* Me'Chell asked the children if they had planted the mushrooms. They said no.

Several weeks passed when Me'Chell started to get sick after she ate. She became suspicious of Thomas, because it only happened when he fixed her something. Me'Chell began to notice the way Thomas looked at her. It was the look of "I wish you were dead." Me'Chell became frightened. "I wonder if Thomas is growing some poisonous mushrooms and using them to poison me." She took some of the mushroom to the police station.

"I found some yellow mushrooms growing in my flower pot, and I was wondering what kind they were.

Can you tell me what they are?" she asked the clerk at the desk.

"I don't know, but we do have a book with just about every kind of mushroom in it. I will get the book, and you can look through it."

The clerk was gone for a short time, and she came back with the mushroom book. Me'Chell and the clerk looked through the book. They found nothing in the book that looked like the mushrooms growing in her flowerpot.

The clerk told Me'Chell, "If you think somebody is doing something to you with these mushrooms, I can take them next door to the detective's office, and they will run tests on them."

"That's okay." They threw the mushrooms in the trash can, and Me'Chell went home, but she did not feel safe after that. She got to the point where she would not eat anything Thomas fixed for her. She would wait until he was gone. If it was a drink, she would pour it out in the sink, and if it was something to eat, she would flush it down the toilet. Me'Chell began to hate coming home. "I have to leave this man. All I feel is hate from him, and it gives me the chills."

Me'Chell became very depressed. When she got home from work, she would fix dinner, and after they ate and the kitchen was cleaned, Me'Chell would lie down on the couch and watch television. Me'Chell's sons became worried about how sad Me'Chell had become.

Tim and Mike were out in the backyard playing. Mike stopped and sat down in a lounge chair. Tim pulled up a chair and sat next to him.

"Tim, have you noticed how sad Mom has gotten?" Mike asked.

"Yes. Mom had not smiled since she married Mr. Thomas. I wish she had not married him. Alfie really loved mom, and we were always doing something together. We had a lot of fun when she was going with Mr. Alfie," Tim remarked.

"Mom has been sad ever since she married Mr. Thomas. She doesn't smile anymore. She doesn't go anywhere. She just lays on the couch and watch television. It's like she has given up, and she's just going through the motions," Mike remarked.

"Yes. I am worried about her. I read up on depression, and Mom has all the symptoms of a depressed person. We need to get Mom out of this house even if it is for a little while," Tim said with great auspice in his voice.

"Let's ask her to take us to the park. Even better, get her to take us to see a movie, something funny. I will get the paper and see what is playing at the movies," Mike stated. He came back with the newspaper.

"I found a good, funny movie. It is *The Pink Panther*. Now let's go and see if we can get Mom to take us to the movie. This movie should make her laugh. Nobody can sit through this movie without laughing," Mike declared. Mike and Tim went into the house. Me'Chell was still on the couch watching television.

"Mom, there is a real good movie playing at the Up Town Movie. It is *The Pink Panther*. We very seldom go anywhere since you got married. We want to go see *The Pink Panther*. Will you take us to the movie?" Mike inquired.

"I don't feel like going anywhere," Me'Chell answered.

"Mom, you owe it to us. We have not had any fun or done any fun things since you got married. This house is depressing. There is no love here. We need to get out of this house," Tim said.

"Maybe we should call Mr. Alfie and ask him to take us to the movie," Mike replied.

"What time is it? The movie probably has already started," Me'Chell remarked.

"The next movie starts in one hour, and we have plenty time if we leave now," Tim blurted out. Me'Chell got up from the couch. "I need to change," Me'Chell stated.

"Mom, you look fine. You don't need to change," Mike said.

"I will leave a note for Thomas and let him know we have gone to the movie," Me'Chell stated.

The boys got a light jacket for them and Me'Chell. "The movie theater is always cold to me," Mike said.

At the theater, they bought some popcorn, candy, and something to drink. The movie had Me'Chell laughing. It was just what the boys wanted, to hear their mother laugh again and to see a smile on her face. They had fun eating the goodies, drinking soda, and laughing. When they got back home, Thomas had not gotten home, but his son was home. He was in the family room stretched out in the lounge chair watching television. Me'Chell and the boys went into the family room and sat down on the couch.

Tim and Mike were still talking and laughing about the movie. Mike said to Thomas's son, "Man, if you want to see a really funny movie go to the Up Town Movie theater and see *The Pink Panther.*"

"Yeah, I heard it was a good movie. Too bad I was not home when you all went to the movie," said Thomas's son with a hostile tone in his voice. Me'Chell went into her bedroom.

"Look, man, we were not trying to leave you out. I don't know if you have noticed how sad Mom has been. She has never smiled or laughed since she married your father. We got her to take us to the movie to bring a smile to her face," Mike explained.

"Yes, Dad is a hard person to live with," Thomas's son blurted out.

Me'Chell came back into the room. "Boys, did you all do your homework?

"Yes. I did my homework at school," Mike answered.

"I did my homework when I first got home," Tim answered.

"Are you all hungry?" she asked.

"I ate a snack when I first got home. Then when we were at the movie, I filled up on all the junk food we had," Mike said.

"And so did I," Tim stated.

Me'Chell turned to Thomas's son. "What about you? Have you eaten dinner?"

"Yes, I have eaten already. Thanks for asking," he replied.

Me'Chell looked at her watch. It was nine o'clock. "I think I will do some reading." Me'Chell picked up the Bible and went into the bedroom. About an hour later, Thomas came home. He came into the bedroom where Me'Chell was. She was lying on the bed reading the Bible.

"What's for dinner?" he asked in a harsh voice.

"What do you mean, what's for dinner? You come home at ten o'clock in the night and have the nerve to ask me what's for dinner? I know you're not expecting for me to get up and fix you something to eat. You mean to tell me they didn't feed you where you just came from? If you are hungry, Thomas, the refrigerator is full of food," Me'Chell snapped.

"Are you trying to get smart with me, woman? I can snap your neck just like that," he said as he snapped his finger. "I don't know why I married you. You are as dumb as I don't know what."

"You know, Thomas, I am tired of you putting me down. I have had it with this marriage. There is no love here. All I see in you is hate for me. I give up on trying to make this thing work. I think it would be best if we get a divorce."

"What are you going to do, go running back to that man?"

"Don't you worry about what I am going to do. One thing's for sure: I'm going to set you free. Then you can find the woman you feel is worthy of you. I am going to bed, and *tomorrow I am going to find a lawyer. Then you won't have* to look at my dumb face too much longer."

CHAPTER 8

Just Want to Be Free

M e'Chell got up early. She gathered up the clothes she was going to wear that day and took them into bathroom. After she took her shower, she got dressed. She was still feeling low. She stood in front of the mirror and looked at herself. *I am not a bad-looking woman, and I am not as dumb as Thomas called me. I have more common sense in my finger then he has in his whole body.* Thomas was just getting up when Me'Chell came out of the bathroom.

"Good morning," he said.

Me'Chell wanted to say, "What's good about it?" but she didn't. "Good morning, Thomas," she responded.

"What are you going to do today?" he asked.

"After I get off work, I think I might go check on my house. This lady keeps worrying me about renting it. I have not been keeping it up like I should, and I need to get someone in the house. I don't know. I have not really thought about it," she answered.

"You want me to check it out for you?"

"No, Thomas. I have not decided what I want or what I am going to do."

Me'Chell got the boys up and fixed breakfast. Thomas, his son, Me'Chell, and her sons sat down at the table and ate breakfast. It was very seldom that they all ate at the same time.

The kids helped clean up the kitchen, and then everybody was off to their destination.

Me'Chell left work early and went to check on her house. She drove by Alfie's business. Deep in her heart, she was hoping to see Alfie. Me'Chell pulled up in front of her house. She got out of the car and went into the house. As she was coming into the house, the phone rang. "What the heck? I thought I had this phone cut off." Me'Chell picked up the phone. "Hello?" Me'Chell called out.

"High stranger," the voce on the other end said.

"Alfie, how did you know I was here?"

"I saw you when you drove by."

"I had this phone cut off. I know I told the phone company to cut it off."

"Is that you biggest worry? I had the phone turned back on."

"Why?"

"Me'Chell, did you know that the boys come up here some times? When they come, they always stop by to see me."

"How did they get up here? We live thirty miles away."

"Most of the time they called me to come and pick them up. I know I should not have, but they were so depressed. Me'Chell, I will always be there for your children. Tim asked me if he could come and stay with me. I told him he would have to ask you."

"You would take in my children? They would live in the beautiful home of yours even if I am married to Thomas?"

"Me'Chell, I love your children just as much as I love you. In the time we spent together, they grew on me. You have some good kids. They need someone to express their anxiety to. We talk, I have taken them out to eat, and I have even taken them to movies. I turned the phone back on for them. Your sons are hurting, Me'Chell. We need to talk. I can't come to your house. Everyone knows how I feel about you, and they would think we were having an affair."

"I don't know."

"There is a building on the corner of Market and Twenty-Fifth Street. Drive into the garage. Park the car, then go to the elevator. Punch in Me'Chell and ALWAYS. The elevator will take you to the right floor. Get off and wait for me. You have to come, Me'Chell. I am worried about you and the boys. They tell me everything."

"Okay," was her answer.

Me'Chell went to the window and peeked around the window shades. She was looking out to see if Thomas was outside checking on her. She did not see his car. But as she walked out of the house, with a glance she checked out the all cars on the street.

Me'Chell got into her car. She kept looking in the mirrors to see if anyone pulled off right after she did. Me'Chell didn't feel safe; she was constantly checking the mirrors.

Finally she reached the destination. She drove into the garage and parked. She waited for a while before getting out of the car. No one had followed her. She got out of the car and went to the elevator like Alfie told her, and punched in Me'Chell and ALWAYS. The elevator door opened and she got in the elevator. There was soft music playing in the elevator. It took her to the third floor. The door opened, and Alfie was standing there waiting for her.

"Hello. You made it," he said.

Me'Chell got out of the elevator, and the greatest desire came over her to fall into Alfie's arms so he could hold her tight, comfort her, make love to her, and make her forget all the misery she had been going through with Thomas.

Alfie reached his hand out to Me'Chell and helped her out of the elevator. As she stepped out of the elevator, the soft music of love was echoing through the hall. It made Me'Chell feel at ease. He took her into one of the rooms. It was an office filled with Mediterranean furniture. There was a large couch by the door. He sat down on the couch. The music was playing in the room as well as the hall.

"Come, Me'Chell. Sit beside me."

Me'Chell's heart was beating fast, and all the passion she could not share with Thomas was now weighing her down. She wanted so badly for Alfie to take her in his arms and make love to her. She sat down beside Alfie, and tears came to her eyes. She held her head down. Alfie took his hand and raised up Me'Chell's head.

"Me'Chell, you know that I love you, don't you?"

"Yes."

"Me'Chell, I would do just about anything for you. It hurts me to know that you are going through so much hell in your marriage. All I want is for you to be happy, and if this man was making you happy, I would not be here now in this room with you. Me'Chell, you have to leave this man. No one should live with someone that treats them the way your husband treats you."

Me'Chell laid her head on Alfie's shoulder and cried. She looked up at Alfie and said, "Alfie, I do love you. I fell in love with you the first night you took me out. Thomas did trick me when he said he would kill himself if I didn't marry him. You don't how many times I wanted to call you, to come to you, and to make love to you. Right now, it is hard being this close to you and not making love to you."

"How do you think I feel? To be this close to you and I can't take you into my arms and make love to you? I want so badly to make love to you, but I will only do that when you become free of your husband. I will not break up your marriage."

"Break up what marriage? All I have been to Thomas is someone to share his bed. I hate my marriage, and I did try to get a divorce once. My lawyer told me I was lucky to be married to Thomas and to go home and work on my marriage. My marriage has been nothing but—"

Alfie put his right hand up to her mouth and said, "I know." Me'Chell kissed his hand.

"Me'Chell, don't. I am just a man, a very weak man right now. I would always feel guilty if I made love to you while you were a married woman."

"Would it be too much to ask you to hold me?"

"No."

Alfie put his arms around Me'Chell, and she leaned down on the couch. Alfie was still holding her. He was now on top of her. His body was shaking. He started to get up. Me'Chell held him tighter. He laid his head on her breast. Me'Chell could feel wetness on her breast. Alfie was crying. After a few minutes, Alfie said, "Me'Chell, I have to let you go. I didn't think it was going to be this hard to be this close to you. I had only planned for us to talk."

Me'Chell took her arms from around him and said, "We haven't done anything except hold each other. I would have felt better if we had gone all the way. I don't want to leave you in this condition."

"Just being close to you makes me feel good, and holding you makes me feel alive. I told you before that I didn't want just your body. I wanted your love. To be able to feel your heart beat, to see you smile when you say my name, and to see my love for you burning in your soul."

"It is said that if a man looks at a woman with lust in his heart, he has already done wrong."

"This was not lust. I look at you with love in my heart."

"Stand up. I want to make sure your clothes don't look like you have been romping around in them."

Me'Chell stood up and straightened her clothes. Her blouse was damp.

"By the time I get home, it will be dry. Alfie, I am not sorry that I came up here. It has been so long since I felt alive and had the fire of passion burning inside of me. Just having you to hold me made me feel like a real woman. I know the kids most likely told you that I have been depressed and walking around sad most of the time. I needed what happened today to bring me back to my old self, to make me feel like a real woman. For that, I thank you."

Soft music filled the room—"I Want To Be Close To You."

"You have never seen me dance. This is for you. All my feeling for you is wrapped up in this song and dance," and she created a dance just for Alfie and her. The song came to an end.

"You are so beautiful, and the dance will always be in my heart, because you made this up just for me." He pushed a button for "I Found Love" to play and took Me'Chell into his arms and they created a dance of love. "Me'Chell, what are you going to do about the way your husband has been treating you?"

"I am going to find another lawyer and get me a divorce."

"Do you need any money?"

"No, I am not going to ask for anything but my freedom. It should not cost much because I am not asking for any support."

Me'Chell felt her blouse, and it was almost dry. "See? I told you it would not take long for my blouse to dry. The song "I Found Love" echoed around the room again. Me'Chell was sitting on the couch. Alfie got on his knees and took Me'Chell's hands and kissed them, and he sang along with the song to her as he kissed her neck, her ear, and then her lips. He got up from his knees and pulled Me'Chell up from the couch, and they danced across the floor. Alfie played "I Want to Be Close to You" again. Me'Chell laid her head on his chest, and they danced to the song. Me'Chell could feel the beats of Alfie's heart, and their hearts beat as one. The song ended, and Me'Chell said, "I'd better be leaving. I want to get home before Thomas gets home from work."

Alfie walked Me'Chell to the elevator. When they got to the elevator, a song by Yolanda Adams "Be Still" came on. Alfie took Me'Chell into his arms and began to sing to her along with the song.

Tears ran down Me'Chell's cheeks, and Alfie kissed away her tears.

"Remember, I will always be there for you. Thanks for coming. I was the one who needed this, to be near you and to hold you once more. Now that I know you are going to get a divorce, I feel so much better. And then you will be all mine. I can't wait to caress you and make sweet love to you."

"There is one thing I want to know, Alfie."

"What is it you want to know?"

"The elevator had my name programmed into it. Like it was waiting for me and knew just where to take me."

"I programmed your name into the elevator when I first met you. You are the only person that is programmed to come up here."

"The person that owns this building let you have the whole floor?"

"I am the person that owns the building. And the answer is no, in case you are wondering if I have ever brought any other woman up here. You are the first and will be the only woman that comes up here."

"You don't act like a person with a lot of money. You are so down-to-earth. You have to be a millionaire. You are good looking and could get any woman you want. Why me? I bet a lot of pretty women have been trying to hook you. You are what women call a good catch."

"I have been looking for someone special. Of all the women I have met, they never had what I wanted in a woman until I saw you. I had already met your family. They showed me a picture of you. Your children always came around and looked at the limos. I kept little snacks in the store. Your children started coming around regularly.

"They would always talk about their mother and how proud they were of you. They talked about your ups and downs, your strength and determination, and then I saw you. You were friendly. You walked by one morning. You looked at me and smiled. Then you said, 'Hello. You have a nice place of business. The way you have your business decorated gives value to the neighborhood.' Your voice was so soft, but sexy. That moment, I fell in love with you and wanted you for my wife. I felt complete. I stood there and watched you walk up the street."

The elevator door opened. The song "Be Still" was still playing. He sang the words, "I will never leave you," and as she was getting into the elevator, tears came to her eyes. Alfie held Me'Chell's hands. She slowly walked backward into the elevator. Her hands slowly eased from Alfie's hands. The words "I will never make you cry" were the words that flowed from his lips as the door closed. When the elevator door open she could see her car sitting in the garage. Me'Chell dried her eyes and walked over to her car. She took her keys from her pants pocket and unlocked the car door and headed home.

It was on that thought that Me'Chell was on while she's now traveling down this road several times returning home from her house. She would pass by a mall, a hotel, and a funeral home that always caught her eyes. Today they were having a funeral at the funeral home. There were lots of cars parked there, but this day something was different. She had driven about a mile from the funeral home when things began to seem like she was in a dream or a fog. She kept driving straight down the road. She drove for about a mile.

She looked to the left of her as she was driving by the funeral home. People were getting into their cars only this time she was on the opposite side of the road. What the heck is going on? I just passed by the funeral home. I never made a left turn, so how did I get on the opposite side of the funeral home heading away from home. She remember feeling like she was in a fog, but never making a left turn to get to the opposite side of the road.

Me'Chell drove to the next corner and turned around, still trying to figure out how she could have gotten to the other side of the road. She droved about a mile looking for the street she wanted to turn on. She must have still been under this fog because she missed the street. She went down to the next block to make the turn. Whose car do you think she saw at the stoplight? It was Thomas. Me'Chell begin to wonder if Thomas had put some kind of spell on her so she would be at that same corner when he got there.

CHAPTER 9

My Heart Belongs to Alfie

When Me'Chell got home, Thomas was not there. Me'Chell got out of the car and checked the mailbox. She took the mail out of the mailbox and went into the house. "Good. I got home first." The kids left a note saying they had gone to the park. "This is even better. Now no one will know what time I got home." She went into the kitchen and washed her hands.

"Now let me see what we are going to have for dinner." Me'Chell looked in the refrigerator. "We are going to have some leftovers tonight." Me'Chell took out some fried chicken and greens. "All I have to do now is cook some cornbread and fix some mashed potatoes." She got some muffin mix and made the bread.

She had just put the bread in the oven when she heard Thomas's car drive up in the driveway. She got the dishes out of the cabinet and set the table. She got some potatoes and washed them. By the time Thomas got in the house, she had finished peeling the potatoes and was cutting them up. The greens and chicken had the kitchen smelling good.

"Hi," Thomas said

"Hello," she answered back.

"What did you do today? Did you go and check on your house?"

"Yes. I went and checked on the house, and everything was fine, so I came home," was her response.

"You mean to tell me you didn't see your old flame?"

"Why would you ask me a question like that? I saw him when I passed by his company. I don't think he saw me. Does that answer your question?"

By the time Me'Chell finished cooking and put the food on the table, the children were home. Everybody washed up for dinner, and they all sat down at the table to eat. Thomas said grace. After they had finish eating, the children helped Me'Chell clean up the kitchen.

"There is a good movie on television tonight," Mike stated.

"What is the movie about?" Me'Chell asked.

"This man and woman fell in love, but he had to go off and fight a war. And her love keeps him going," answered Mike.

"I don't what to see no love story," Thomas replied.

"It is more than a love story. It is a story about a soldier trying to stay alive with bullets flying all around him. And when he thinks he is not going to make it, he thinks about what is waiting back home for him. This makes him a fighting machine. He not only saves his life, but he saves his whole company. And he comes home a hero. I can't tell you any more about the movie. You will have to watch it to see how it ends. There are quite a few good movies on tonight," Mike stated.

"I don't mind watching it if there is not a lot of mushy stuff in it," Tim said.

Me'Chell spoke up and said, "Well, I will go along with whatever you all want to watch."

"I am going into the game room. You all can watch whatever," Thomas stated.

Thomas's son said, "I think I would like the war movie."

"Okay. Tim, are you going to watch television with us?" Mike asked.

"I don't care as long as it is a good movie," Tim answered. They all gathered in the family room. Me'Chell made some popcorn. As Me'Chell watched the movie, her mind drifted back to when she and Alfie were together.

All she could think of was how good it felt to be held by Alfie and how his kiss sent fire though her soul. Now her body was aching for him. *I have to get my divorce. I love Alfie, and he loves me. Thomas doesn't appreciate me. I need to feel loved. He never loved me. He just could not stand someone else loving me. What kind of man would marry a person just to keep them from a person that really loves them?* These thoughts were running around in her mind.

Before she knew it, the movie was over. Even though she was looking at the movie, she did not see it. Her mind was far away from the movie. All she could think about was Alfie and the fire he had ignited in her soul.

Me'Chell got up and said, "That was a good movie. I think I am going to turn in for the night. Good night, everyone."

She went into the bedroom. Thomas was in bed watching the television.

"How was the movie?" he asked.

"It was a good movie. It was sad, funny, and had a lot of drama in it."

Me'Chell went into the bathroom. *He is in the bed waiting for me to get in the bed. He is going to want to have sex. How can I have sex with him tonight, of all nights? My heart right now is with Alfie. My body is not going to respond to him. I guess I could give him what he wants and make-believe he is Alfie. Maybe I should go back in the family room and watch television until he goes to sleep,* Me'Chell thought. *No, that is not going to work. He will wake up as soon as I get into the bed. I will have to be careful and not call out Alfie's name.*

Me'Chell messed around as long as she could in the bathroom. Me'Chell had been in the bathroom for one hour. She was hoping that Thomas would be asleep when she got into bed. Me'Chell carefully turned the covers on her side of the bed back so she could ease into the bed, hoping not to wake Thomas. She got as close to the edge of the bed as she could.

"I thought you were going to spend the night in the bathroom. I was wondering when you were going to come to bed. What took you so long in the bathroom?"

"I gave myself a facial."

Thomas pulled Me'Chell close to him. Then he started to pull up her gown. This is what she had dreaded. Thomas wanted to have sex, and her feelings for him were gone. In fact, Me'Chell lost that loving feeling for Thomas shortly after they were married. She laid there as he rubbed his hands over her legs. All she felt was chills that made her want to scream. She felt his body getting on top of her. To her, this was as bad as being raped, because she didn't want to have sex with him. *All my feelings for him are gone.* He tried to kiss her. She moved her head.

I have to get this man off me. I can't stand this. She felt like crying. *Please hurry and get this over with*, she kept thinking. *Maybe if I think I am making love to Alfie, I can get him off me quicker.* Me'Chell let her mind drift back to when she and Alfie were on the couch. She thought about how he made her feel and the fire of passion that consumed her. She was living that moment in her mind, only now she was going all the way with him.

Finally, Thomas had finished what he married her for. Me'Chell thought, *I have to get out of this marriage…like yesterday! I can't stand for him to touch me. If I hold back on him, he is going to think I am having an affair. I have to go see a lawyer tomorrow and get my divorce started. There is no way I can have him fumble over me like this.*

Thomas got up before Me'Chell. When she woke up, he had already taken his bath and was coming out of the bathroom.

"Good morning," he said, breaking the silence.

"Good morning, Thomas," Me'Chell responded.

"Are you going to get up now?"

"Yes. I want to get to work early today."

"What is so important about today? What are you going to do today?"

"I don't have anything planned. I am trying to be the first one to work. Everybody else can come to work late, and they never get written up, but if I am two minutes late, I get written up. If I get to work first, I will write it down in my handbook. I am going to keep a record of who comes in late and what is done about it."

"Do you want me to help you make the bed?"

"Yes, I would like that," Me'Chell answered.

Thomas helped Me'Chell make up the bed. Me'Chell gathered up the clothes she was going to wear to work and went into the bathroom.

"I might be late coming home this evening." Thomas muttered.

"Okay," Me'Chell called out.

Me'Chell finished her bath and did her morning routine. Then she got dressed for work. She went into the kitchen, and the boys were eating breakfast. Thomas had already left for work. Me'Chell fixed some oatmeal. Thomas had fixed some coffee that had the house smelling good. Me'Chell got a cup of coffee and sat down at the table with the boys.

"Do you all have anything special to do today?" she asked.

"No. Well, I would like to stay after school and watch the basketball practice," Mike answered.

"If Mike stays after school and watch the practice, I want to also stay," Tim uttered.

"In other words, you all will need someone to pick you up from school?"

"Mom, you are so smart. We will need a ride home after practice."

"Okay. I will come and get you."

"I am glad those days are over for me," Thomas' son said.

After they had finished eating, they cleaned up the kitchen. Me'Chell's boys got their coats and ran out the door. They did not want to miss their bus. Me'Chell got her coat and purse. She checked to see if her keys were in it. She took the keys out of her purse and went into the garage where she had park her car yesterday. Me'Chell very seldom parks her car in the garage. She told herself she did it to make Thomas think she had not gotten home, then to see his face when he walked into the kitchen and saw her fixing dinner.

CHAPTER 10

Yours Forever

It was the same old, same old at work for Me'Chell. She was working her "you know what" off while other people were goofing off. *I don't know how some people can leave their work for others to do, yet they get all the glory in this place. I have too much to think about today to worry about these people. I can't wait until I get my lunch break. I am going to find a lawyer about getting my divorce from Thomas.*

Time was going by so slowly for Me'Chell. Finally, it was time for her to take her lunch break. Me'Chell went to the pay phone at the Sub Shop next door. Looking through the phonebook, she found several divorce lawyers.

There was one that stood out from the others. She dialed her number. *I am going to get a woman lawyer. She could better understand what I am going through than a man lawyer.*

"This is Dickerson and Dickerson Law Firm," the voice on the other end of the phone said.

"I would like to see attorney Ellen Dickerson about getting a divorce. Can you give me an appointment at noon tomorrow? Good. Thank you." Me'Chell hung up the phone and went up to the counter and ordered a sandwich. She sat down at a table. "Now I have to see how I am going to put in for a divorce without Thomas knowing it until I find a place to move." She called Alfie and told him that she had an appointment tomorrow with Ellen Dickerson at noon. After Me'Chell finished eating, she went back to work.

The rest of the day went by fast. *I have to start looking for a place to live. I have to be careful not to give any signs that I am going to leave him. Thomas is so territorial, and I don't know what he would do to me if he found out before I moved.*

Me'Chell went home after work and tried to act normal, but Thomas could sense that something was different about the way Me'Chell was acting.

"Are you all right Me'Chell?"

"Yes, why do you ask?"

"I don't know. You seem to be deep in thought. I was just wondering what was on your mind."

"I was just thinking about work today. How some of my coworkers can get away with not doing their part of the work. This means I end up doing their job as well as mine. I do most of the work, and they get the pay raises."

"I hope you are not making stink about it. They worked there long before you started working there."

"No, I am not. I have not put in any complains, but it would be nice to see you take my side some time. How would you feel if one of your coworkers did not do his part of the work, but he was getting raises and you were not?"

"You sound a little petty to me. I don't think that person would have gotten a raise if he did not do a good job at work."

That was close. He has already detected that I am planning something. I hope what I told him about work will satisfy his curiosity.

Me'Chell fixed dinner, and after she set the table, she called out "Dinner is ready!"

Thomas's son had not gotten home after dinner, and when the kitchen was cleaned, the boys went outside to play. Me'Chell was trying to be her old self. She turned on the television. She searched the channels until she found something that Thomas liked.

"Thomas, there is a good movie on, *The Gun Slingers.* Do you want to watch it?"

"No, I am going to read the paper. I think you watch too much television. You should read more."

Me'Chell was glad Thomas did not want to watch the movie. Now until bedtime, she did not have to worry about being around Thomas. But how was she going to handle bedtime? The boys soon came back into the house.

"What are you watching? This looks like it might be good."

"Yes, it is good. Have you all done your homework?"

"Mom, we did our homework when we first got home. We knew that you were going to be on our back about the homework. We always do our homework when we first get home, or we do it at school. Then we won't have to have you getting on our backs."

"You all are such good boys."

Me'Chell heard the front door open. It was Thomas's son. He walked in the family room. "Hello. Where is Dad?"

"He is in bedroom reading," Me'Chell answered.

"Are you hungry? Me'Chell asked.

"Yes, I am. I was not able to make it home for dinner."

"I can fix you something to eat," Me'Chell offered.

"No, that's all right. I can find something to eat. I don't want you to miss any of the movie."

"We do have a television in the kitchen, so it would not be a problem," Me'Chell replied.

"I know, but I can find something to eat."

Thomas's son went into the kitchen and fixed himself something to eat. Before Me'Chell knew it, the news was on, and the time for her to go to bed was near. After the news went off, Me'Chell went into the bedroom.

Thomas was already in bed. Me'Chell walked very softly, hoping not to wake her beloved husband. Thomas turned over in the bed and said, "That must have been a really good movie."

"Yes, it was, and after the movie ended, I watched the news. They are talking about gas going up again. It seems like there is something always going up," Me'Chell stated as she yawned.

Damn, I was hoping he would be asleep by now. She got her gown and went into the bathroom. She didn't stay in there long. She was afraid it might make Thomas curious and get him thinking she didn't want to be with him anymore. And if he started thinking, she didn't want him; the next thing that would come to his mind was she wanted to leave him. *I want to get a divorce. Tomorrow I will see the lawyer about getting a divorce from Thomas. I will also look for a place to move to.*

Me'Chell came out of the bathroom. Thomas was sitting up in bed.

"I like that gown on you," he said.

"Thanks," Me'Chell answered. She knew what he was waiting for. He always said something nice when he wanted to have sex. She got into the bed. Thomas pulled her closed to him and began to caress her. Me'Chell got up and pulled off her gown. *I hope he make this quick*, she said to herself.

She hated every minute of it and tried to act like she was enjoying his moment of what he called making love. This was tearing her apart. She had lost all feeling for Thomas, and having sex with him was like being raped by a stranger. Then the moment came that she was praying for. He had finished.

Me'Chell waited until he had gone to sleep, and she went into the bathroom and washed up.

Me'Chell went back to bed and lay on her side. Her back was facing Thomas, and in silence, she cried herself to sleep.

When she woke up, Thomas was already up. He had showered and was getting dressed.

"Good morning, Me'Chell."

"Good morning, Thomas."

"What are you going to do today?" he asked.

"The only thing I have planned today is to go to work. Why? Do you something planned for this evening?" she responded.

"No. I don't have anything planned."

Thomas went into the kitchen. Me'Chell's boys were coming out of their bedroom, and they went into the kitchen.

"Good morning, Mr. Thomas," they both said.

"Good morning, boys. I hope you had a good night's sleep. A good night's sleep is important to get you through the day. How is school coming along with you all?"

"School is good. My grades are good," Mike responded.

"Same here. Everything is fine. Thanks for asking," Tim said.

Me'Chell came in to the kitchen. "I will have breakfast fixed in just a minute," Me'Chell stated. Me'Chell fixed some grits, bacon, and eggs for breakfast. After everybody had eaten, Mike and Tim helped clean up the kitchen. Thomas's son came into the kitchen.

"What's for breakfast?" he asked.

"There are some grits in the pot on the stove and some bacon in the microwave. If you want me to, I can fix you some eggs."

"No, that's all right. I will just eat me some cornflakes," he muttered.

"Okay, then I will put up the bacon and pour out the rest of the grits, and I can finish cleaning up the kitchen," Me'Chell replied. Me'Chell had to hurry and finish cleaning up the kitchen or she would be late for work. And that was one thing she did not want to be. She had a lot of personal things she had to take care of today, like seeing the lawyer and filing for a divorce. She also had to find a place to stay.

Me'Chell looked at the clock. She only had forty minutes to get to work and clock in. It took her about a half an hour to get to work. Then she had to find a parking space and get clock in. "I can make it on time if I don't have to hunt for a parking space," she said to herself. She was lucky there was a parking spot close to the building. She parked and hurried into the building. Just as she clocked in, the clock struck eight o'clock. She had made it just in time.

Eagerly, she went about doing her job. "I can't let these people get on my nerves today. I have to have a clear head." She kept watching the clock.

The hour she had been so anxiously waiting for had arrived: her lunch break. Me'Chell rushed out of the building and got into her car. She only had an hour to get to the lawyer's office, file for a divorce, and get back to work on time. "I hope this lawyer doesn't make me wait on her." When she got to the lawyer's office, the secretary sent her to the lawyer's room.

"Hello, Mrs. Thomas. Have a seat and tell me why you want to get a divorce," the lawyer said.

"I want to get a divorce because I am being mentally and physically abused." Me'Chell told the lawyer how Thomas had been treating her. She also told her not to serve him the divorce papers until she found a place to stay, because she was afraid of Thomas," Me'Chell stated. Me'Chell looked at her watch. She only had twenty minutes left of her lunch break. She had just enough time for her to get back to work and not be late. But first, she had to call Alfie and let him know she did talk to the lawyer about getting the divorce and to thank him for paying the lawyer. The lawyer told Me'Chell that a man named Alfie called and said he would pay for her divorce.

"Can I use your phone to make a call?" she asked the lawyer.

"Yes. You can use the phone," answered the lawyer.

She dialed Alfie's number. She knew she did not have time to talk to Alfie, but she had to let him know she had filed for the divorce. Alfie answered the phone.

"Alfie, yes, I did see the lawyer today, and thanks for paying her. Now I have to find a place fast so I can move out of that house. I don't want you to buy me a house. I will find a place before the week is over. And then I can be with the man I love and the one that loves me—you, Alfie. I have to go. I don't want to be late going back to work."

Me'Chell hung up the phone and hurried back to work. She had spent her lunch break at the lawyer's office and was not able to get anything to eat.

The rest of the day went by without a problem, except that her stomach kept telling her it wanted some food. Me'Chell was wondering how she was going to pull everything off without making Thomas suspicious. She hurried back to work and was able to clock in on time.

Me'Chell went about doing her work and got no complaints from anyone.

So far, the day has gone well. I hope that when I get home, everything will go as well, she thought to herself.

Her shift had ended, and she was on her way home, praying that she would be able to pull everything off before Thomas found out she was leaving him. As Me'Chell was coming down the street they lived on, she could see Thomas's car in the driveway. *I wonder what Thomas is doing home so early*, were the thoughts that ran through her mind. Me'Chell pulled up into the driveway and parked behind Thomas's car.

She got out of the car and went into the house. Thomas was in the kitchen fixing dinner. *That's strange*, she thought. Thomas *never cooks. I wonder what he is up to.*

"Hi, Me'Chell," he greeted her with a smile on his face.

"Hi. Are you cooking dinner? What brought you home early today?"

"Oh, nothing special. I just felt like doing something different today."

"But you have never left work early or cooked dinner."

Thomas had some sauce in a pan; he was stirring it. He put some on a spoon. He wanted Me'Chell to taste it.

"Taste this sauce and see if I have enough spice in it."

Me'Chell walked over to the stove where Thomas was standing. He held the spoon up to her mouth. Me'Chell's gut feeling was telling her not to taste that stuff.

"First, what are you trying to make? It smells awful. I'm not going to taste something if I don't like the way it smells. Do you want me to help you finish cooking?"

"No. I want to do this myself."

"Okay then, I'm going into the bedroom. If you need anything, just call me."

Me'Chell went into the bedroom. Her mind was wandering. *What's up with this man today? Can he be onto me or have somebody watching me? If he knows I went to see a lawyer today, there's no telling what is on his mind. I have to find a place fast.* Me'Chell could hear the boys. Her boys were home. *I will have to go out there and make-believe that nothing is wrong. Tomorrow I am going to find a place even if I have to go to a hotel. What am I going to tell the boys?*

If I walk out of here tomorrow and move into a hotel, I will have to somehow get to the boys before they get on the school bus to come home. They will not be able to come back and get their things. I know that they are not going to like that. Me'Chell went into the kitchen. Thomas had the table set and the food was on the table. The boys were in the backyard.

"I have dinner ready. You need to call Mike and Tim to come and eat," Thomas said.

Me'Chell went to the door and called the boys to come in and clean up for dinner. They came into the house and went into the bathroom and washed their hands. After dinner Me'Chell and the boys cleaned up the kitchen. Thomas's son and some of his friends had gone on a camping trip and would not be back for a week.

Me'Chell thought she could leave work early and come back while Thomas was at work and get the boys and some of her things. That night, Me'Chell was restless. She had so much on her mind.

"Are you all right?" Thomas asked.

"Yes. Why do you ask me that question?"

"You have been a little distant lately. Are you sure you don't have something to tell me?"

"Tell you? Like what?"

"That is what I would like to know."

"All I can tell you is I am tried, and I think I will go to bed."

"It is still early. It's only eight o'clock. I think I will stay up and do some reading." Thomas replied.

Me'Chell went into the bedroom and took a shower. After she said her prayers, she got into bed. When she woke up it was morning. But something was not right. She did not feel good. Thomas was up and dressed.

"Good morning, Me'Chell."

"Good morning, Thomas." As she tried to get out of bed, a sharp pain hit her hard in her chest.

Thomas looked at her. "Are you okay?" he asked.

"Yes. I am fine," she answered. The pain showed on her face. "Maybe you should stay home today. You look like you are in a lot of pain."

"I will be all right when I get some fresh air." She sat on the edge of the bed until Thomas left.

Why am I hurting like this? It was a struggle for her to go to the bathroom and get ready for work. *It's a good thing I took a bath last night.* It seemed like hours to Me'Chell for her to get ready for work. When she came out of the bedroom, everybody was gone. She looked at the clock and realized she was going to be late for work. She tried to eat some corn flakes, but the pain would not let her eat. *How am I going to get to work? If I can't eat, how can I drive to work? I have to get out of here.*

I have so much to do today. Me'Chell went outside to her car. She got in the car and leaned back on the seat. She rolled down the window and sat in the car for a while. The fresh air seemed to make her feel better.

Me'Chell was an hour late for work that morning. When she walked into the office, everyone looked at her.

"Me'Chell, this is the first time you have been late. You don't look too good," her supervisor commented.

"I am all right. I just need to sit down for a little while."

"I told everybody you must be sick because you are never late, and you don't take unauthorized time off. You are a very dependable person."

All this time, she thought her supervisor didn't notice how hard she worked or that she was always on time. "I don't know what to say," Me'Chell responded.

"You just sit here for a while, and if you don't feel better in about twenty minutes you might need to go to the doctor," her supervisor said with concern.

The supervisor left and came back with some ginger ale. "Me'Chell, drink this ginger ale and see if it will help you any." Me'Chell drank the ginger ale.

"Can I use the phone?" she asked the supervisor.

"Sure you can. Here, let me bring it over to you. I have to go check on a few things. I will be back as soon as I can and see how you are doing." Me'Chell called Alfie.

He answered the phone.

"Alfie, I think Thomas knows about me leaving. When I got home yesterday, he was home. Ether he is watching me or has someone else watching me, and for the first time, he fixed dinner. When I walked into the kitchen, he was cooking dinner. He had some sauce he wanted me to taste, but I told him I didn't like the way it smelled so I didn't taste it. This morning when I woke up, I had a sharp pain in my chest. I don't know how I made it to work. I had to get out of that house."

This frightened Alfie. He told her not to go back to the house. "Thomas is not going to let you leave him alive. I will have a place for you to go by the time you leave work. There is a house near your job for sale. I already talked to the owner about buying it."

"Alfie, I don't want you to buy me a house. You already bought it, and you are going to make sure it will be ready for me by this evening? Alfie, I am at work, and I have to get off the phone. I will call you before I leave work."

The pain in her chest had eased up. The supervisor came back into the office. "You look better, Me'Chell. Do you want to go home or stay at work?"

"I am going to stay." On her lunch break, Me'Chell went to a pay phone in the building and called Alfie.

"Alfie, I feel better now. I will leave tomorrow. I will leave like I am going to work then I will come back home and get the boys' things. I know you love me, and I love you too. I can't wait to get out of this marriage so we can be together. I will try to call you later. If not, I will call you tomorrow morning. I love you. Okay, 'bye."

Me'Chell had spent her whole lunch break talking to Alfie. Now it was time for her to go back to work. By the time her shift had ended, all the pain in her chest was gone. When Me'Chell got home, Mike and Tim were in the family room.

Thomas had not gotten home. Me'Chell got the boys and took them outside in the yard, away from the house. She didn't trust that the house and patio weren't bugged.

"I am planning on leaving Thomas tomorrow, but he does not know it. I want you all to call Alfie tomorrow, and he will tell you where to go. Please don't let Thomas know. I don't trust him. Alfie and I think he would try to hurt me if he knew I was going to leave."

"What about our stuff?" asked Tim.

"What is more important to you, your stuff or my life? I am going to try to come home early and get as much of your things as I can. I think Thomas already knows that something is up, so please act like nothing has changed."

Me'Chell and the boys went back into the house. Me'Chell went into the kitchen and started on the dinner. By the time Thomas got home, Me'Chell had the table set and dinner was ready to be served. After dinner, Mike and Tim helped Me'Chell clean up the kitchen; then, they went to their bedroom. Once in their room, Tim started to put things that were most important to him in his backpack.

"You have too much stuff in your bag. With all that stuff, how are you going to get your books in it?"

"I still can get my book in my bag. Plus Mr. Thomas will be gone when the school bus comes to pick us up.

When I get to school, I will put this stuff in my locker," Tim answered.

Me'Chell went into the family room to watch television. Thomas watched television with her for a little while; then, he said, "Tomorrow is going to be a busy day for me. I think I will go to bed early." Me'Chell waited until she thought Thomas was asleep. She turned off the television and went into the bedroom.

She went into the bathroom and brushed her teeth. She looked at the toothpaste. "This is not the same brand that I use, and I don't like the way it tastes." Me'Chell put some water in a glass and rinsed out her mouth. She put on her night clothes and went to bed. In the middle of the night, Me'Chell's chest and stomach started to hurt. She got up and went into the bathroom and took some medicine for her upset stomach and went back to bed.

Thomas was up before her as usual. He came out of the bathroom and spoke to Me'Chell.

"Good Morning, Me'Chell. You were a little restless last night."

"I started feeling bad, so I got up and took some medicine. I feel fine now. I guess I had better get up and get ready for work," she responded.

She took her shower and got dressed for work. The boys were sitting at the table eating some cereal.

"Good morning, boys. I see you all have already started on your breakfast. If you want some pancakes or eggs, I can fix them for you. The bus is not coming for at least a half hour."

"Thanks, Mom, but we are fine. Mr. Thomas has gone to work already," Tim said.

Me'Chell changed the subject. She was afraid that he might say something about her leaving Thomas. Me'Chell was suspicious about Thomas and thought that he had the house bugged. After the boys left, Me'Chell was putting the dishes in the dishwasher, and she started to get sick. "I have to get out of this house. It is making me sick."

Me'Chell got her car keys and went out to her car. As she got in the car, she got hot and started to sweat. She had only gotten a few blocks from her house when she pulled her car over to the curb and got out of the car. There was a store a block up the street. Me'Chell got back into her car and drove to the store. She sat in the parking lot for a while.

"I don't think I can make it to work. I will call Alfie and let him know I am going back to the house." Me'Chell went into the store. There was a phone near the door. Me'Chell called Alfie.

"Alfie, I don't think I can make it to work. I am going to go back home and go to bed. I feel so bad. Like my heart is going to jump out of my chest. You think whatever is wrong with me, Thomas had something to do with it? Maybe I will go to the doctor. I told the boys to call you when they get out of school. I had planned on leaving Thomas today. You don't want me to go back to the house? I am going to be fine. Alfie, I am going to be fine. Thomas is not home. He went to work early this morning. I will be out of the house before he gets home. I love you."

Me'Chell hung up the phone and drove back to the house. She pulled up in the driveway and pressed the garage door opener. Thomas's car was in the garage.

What is he doing home? she thought. I can't leave; I know he heard the garage door open. He knows I'm home. Me'Chell closed the door and got out of the car. Me'Chell went into the house. Thomas was sitting in the bedroom watching television.

"Hi, Thomas. You didn't go to work today?" she asked.

"No. I thought I would stay home and just take it easy today," he answered.

"When did you decide to stay home? You left for work early this morning."

"What difference does it make when I made up my mind to stay home. What brings you back home?"

"I was not feeling good. I got halfway to work, and I almost passed out. I feel better now. Maybe I will go to work anyway."

Me'Chell went into the family room and sat on the couch. She was getting weaker, not better. Thomas came into the family room.

"Me'Chell, I have to go to the store. Do you want me to bring you anything?"

"No. I am going to be fine."

As soon as Thomas's car pulled out, Me'Chell called Alfie.

"Alfie, I am not going to be able to leave today. I am so sick. I feel like I am getting weaker."

Alfie knew something was wrong. Me'Chell should not have gotten that sick in such a short time. He was afraid that Thomas was doing something to make her sick, even to the point of killing her.

"If I don't feel better in a couple of hours, I am going to call an ambulance to take me to the hospital."

Me'Chell hung the phone and lay down on the couch. She was getting weaker. Two hours had passed and Thomas had not returned home. The phone rang. Me'Chell tried to get up from the couch. Her body did not want to move. She fell to the floor and dragged herself to the phone.

"Hello?" was the soft and shaky voice of Me'Chell. "Alfie, I can't get up. I feel like I am dying. Yes, please call an ambulance to take me to the hospital. When I get to the hospital, I know I will get better." Alfie had tears in his eyes. He was afraid they waited too long to get Me'Chell to the hospital. He told Me'Chell he was coming to the hospital, and he did not care about Thomas seeing him there. He was going to tell Thomas that he was going to take Me'Chell home with him.

Alfie thought back to when he told Me'Chell, "It seems like every time you want to go more than twenty miles from the house, you always get sick." Thomas was doing something to her, and Thomas was not going to let her leave him. He could not stand the fact that another man would love her. He believed Thomas would rather see her dead first.

Me'Chell's weak voice saying, "My heart is beating so fast. I feel like I am going to have a heart attack," brought Alfie back to the reality that his greatest fear was now real. "I am so weak I don't think I can hold the phone any longer."

"Hold on, Me'Chell. The ambulance is on the way." He started to sing to her their favorite songs. "When I Found You," "I Found Love," and "I Just Want to Be Close to You."

Alfie heard the sound of the phone falling. "Me'Chell! Me'Chell! Pick up the phone!" he called out in panic.

Thomas return home and walked into the room and saw the phone off the hook and Me'Chell lying on the floor near the couch. The doorbell was buzzing. He went to the door. The EMTs were at the door. Thomas opened the door and let them in.

"We got a call about a women being sick."

"Yes, my wife is sick. She is on the floor, and I don't think she is breathing."

One of the EMTs checked on her. "She is not breathing," he called out and started CPR on her. Alfie was listening to all that was going on and tears were rolling down his face. He knew that she was dead. Thomas picked up the phone. "Who is this on the phone?"

"I am from the public TV station, and I was talking to the lady of the house about a donation. She stopped talking, and it sounded like she dropped the phone. Is she okay?"

"No, I think my wife is dead. I have to hang up now."

Alfie hung up the phone and started to cry. "Why did I let her go back to that man? I knew he was not going to let her get a divorce. I told her Thomas would rather see her dead than to let her leave him. Me'Chell, why didn't you believe me? You know that I loved you and wanted to marry you. I would have given you anything you wanted. You told me that his first wife died of a heart attack, and she also wanted a divorce. I was afraid the same would happen to you, and I was right."

Alfie watched the paper to see what funeral home was handling her funeral. Two days after he had talked to her, he saw her obituary in the paper. He cut her picture out of the paper and put it in a frame. Then he picked up the phone and called the funeral home.

"Hello. My name is Alfie, and I am a friend of Me'Chell Thomas. I see you have her body. I would like to come down and see her. I know, but I need a favor. I should have been the man she married, and I don't want to start any tension, so what I want to do is come down when no one else is there. I will pay you whatever you want for your extra time. Good. I will be there at 9:00 tonight. Thanks."

Alfie showed up at 9:00 on the dot. They took him into a room where Me'Chell's body was. Alfie had a red rose in his hand, and he placed it over her heart.

"Me'Chell, I warned you. If only you had left the day you signed your divorce papers." He touched her hands, and it felt normal, not like a dead person's icy cold hard. He leaned over and kissed her hands and tears flowed from his eyes.

"I will never love anyone but you. I will love you until the day I die," he said through his tears. Me'Chell, my precious love."

The manager of the funeral home came into the room. "Come with me," he said.

Alfie got up and went with the manager. "Sit here and let me get you something to drink. Do you like coffee?"

"Yes."

"Do you take cream or sugar in your coffee?"

"Black."

"You are taking Me'Chell's death very hard, and I want you to calm down before leaving here."

"I wanted to marry Me'Chell, and that man tricked her into marrying him. He never loved her, and I loved her with all my heart. He killed her. I don't know how he did it. That heart attack was a man-made heart attack. She never had anything wrong with her heart."

"You have to be careful what you say. If he finds out you are saying these things about him, he could sue you, unless you have proof."

"Thanks for the time and the coffee."

Alfie went to Me'Chell's funeral. She still had the red rose over her heart, and she looked like she was sleeping. On Me'Chell's birthdays and all holidays, he went to Me'Chell's grave and put a red rose on her grave. A tear would fall from his eyes as he sat there and played some of her favorite music—"It's Not for Me to Say" and "I Found Love When I Found You." Mike and Tim moved in with Alfie. They went to college and were successful in everything they did.

You can contact me to order more book of

Married to the Wrong Man

Please Print name _____

Address _____

City_____ State_____ Zip _____

Phone ( ) _____

_____ copies of book @ 19.99 each $ _____

P & H @ $ 5.00 per book $ _____

Total amount enclosed $ _____

Make check or money order payable to:
M. Louise Davis

Send order to:
M. Louise Davis
P. O. Box 634* Colonial Heights, VA 23834

Lightning Source UK Ltd.
Milton Keynes UK
UKOW07f1935141214

243121UK00013B/160/P